Cade's breath came out in a rush. "You're playing with fire, darlin'."

Emma couldn't help but agree. Heat rushed up her neck and down through her belly.

This man was sin incarnate, her personal temptation in every way, from his boots to his jeans to his very, *very* fine body. Everything about him appealed to her. Even his stubbornness.

She'd never experienced this crazy rush of desire, the raw cravings that had her wanting to accept his stupid challenge and see what two weeks would bring. Particularly if it meant seduction and touching and... She shivered.

Then she smiled, rubbing her cheek against his, leaving a slight whisker burn against her skin. "Don't think I don't know exactly what I'm doing, *darlin'*."

She pressed closer, her lips brushing the shell of his ear.

"You have no idea what I'm capable of...or just how good at it I might be..."

Dear Reader,

Welcome to the second book in the Wild Western Heat series, where the New Mexico plains heat up with more than sunshine.

Cowboy Proud is the story of Cade, the second Covington brother. Cade believes that love isn't worth the heartache it inevitably brings. Until he meets the woman who is his complete opposite—city to his country, slick to his rough, polished to his unpolished. But it's their very differences that fuel the fires of a passion neither could have dreamed they'd ever find, particularly in each other.

Having lived on a ranch in New Mexico, so much of this brings home beautiful memories of my time there. The country there is unbelievable, ranging from plains to sand hills, barren desert to stunning mountains, tiny creeks to pristine, trout-filled waters and more. It's truly one of the most beautiful and diverse places in the United States.

And, as I've said before, New Mexico cowboys are every bit as sexy and sincere as those neighboring Texas cowboys. I should know—I married one.

Until next time, happy reading!

Kelli Ireland

Kelli Ireland

——

Cowboy Proud

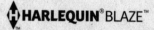

HARLEQUIN® BLAZE™

ISBN-13: 978-0-373-79878-0

Cowboy Proud

Printed in U.S.A.

Kelli Ireland spent a decade as a name on a door in corporate America. Unexpectedly liberated by Fate's sense of humor, she chose to carpe the diem and pursue her passion for writing. A fan of happily-ever-afters, she found she loved being the puppet master for the most unlikely couples. Seeing them through the best and worst of each other while helping them survive the joys and disasters of falling in love? Best. Thing. Ever. Visit Kelli's website at kelliireland.com.

Books by Kelli Ireland

Harlequin Blaze

Pleasure Before Business

Stripped Down
Wound Up
Pulled Under

Wild Western Heat

A Cowboy Returns

This book wouldn't have happened if not for Gina Lamm, fellow author and friend, encourager and taskmaster.

Your creativity and drill-sergeant-like ways are absolutely amazing.

I'll drop and give you twenty if this book doesn't live up to its potential. I promise.

1

THE BLACK, HORSESHOE-SHAPED bootjack sat just inside the front door. It served as a subtle but unmistakable reminder to all who entered the Bar C's main house that cowboy boots came off *right there*. If the boots, or the cowboy in them, went any farther than the foyer, that cowboy would find himself wielding a broom and a mop, courtesy of the lady of the house.

Cade Covington notched his left boot heel in the jack and tugged his foot free, repeating the action with his right. Standing in his stocking feet, age-old instinct had him looking down to see if they had holes. The action made him grin unexpectedly, as memories settled over him, thin as late-morning mist.

Not since his mother died more than nineteen years ago had shoe removal been a house rule. But Reagan Matthews had resurrected it the moment she'd moved in with the eldest Covington son and Cade's older brother, Elijah. Didn't matter that the house was owned equally by all three brothers. Reagan had taken over the majority of the household chores and thereby set the place to rights as only a woman ever could, turning house into home, and she'd lain down the law.

Cade had grumbled at the time because his easy acceptance would've been suspect. It was no secret he resented change, particularly in his personal life. But his dislike of mopping floors far exceeded "resentment." He *hated* that particular chore. So he'd deal with this particular change.

The major ranch renovations were a different story. His personal comfort level was currently parked in another county—in a neighboring state, in fact. The project was almost done, and as soon as the last nail was driven and the last plant planted, the results would set in motion massive, unimaginable changes in everyone's lives.

Cade had gone along with the initial suggestions months ago as a last-ditch effort to keep Eli involved in the ranch again, as a desperate measure to reestablish the lost relationship with his older brother, as an effort to fill the aching void Eli's absence had wrought when he'd left the ranch years ago.

And there was also the money aspect. The three brothers and Reagan, at her insistence, had taken out a mortgage on the ranch. Land they'd owned free and clear, land that had been in the Covington family since before New Mexico had officially been a state, now held a million-dollar-plus mortgage on it.

The idea brought Cade to an unsteady stop. *A million dollars*. He'd never thought to see that kind of dollar figure attached to his name in any way, let alone as debt. Always the brother most focused on fiscal security, his hand had shaken so hard at the bank signing, he'd screwed up the paperwork. Twice. But it was done. Finding another way forward wasn't an option anymore. No, his "option" was more do-or-be-damned "obligation." The Bar C would be a successful dude ranch or they'd lose it all. Forcing himself to stand, Cade continued through the living room and headed for the kitchen, stockinged feet padding softly over worn hardwood floors.

Food first. Worry later.

If he was lucky, Reagan might have packaged the leftover enchiladas she'd made for dinner last night. She was awesome about stuff like that, the nurturing, thinking ahead, meal planning. All that and more, really. After his old man died, when it had just been Cade and his younger brother, Tyson, living at the house, mealtimes had been fend-for-yourself events. They'd considered it a good day if they came up with something that couldn't be mistaken for a mold culture, wasn't seriously outdated or hadn't suffered such severe freezer burn it was rendered unrecognizable. Survival had depended greatly on peanut butter sandwiches or, if either of them finished their day and wasn't too tired to boil water, one man might have put in the effort to cook spaghetti noodles and open a can of eighty-eight-cent sauce. Those days were over, though.

One change that's been pretty good overall...

He grinned and shook his head. Keep up that kind of positive attitude and people would begin to wonder if he'd suffered a head injury. Not that he was negative, just realistic. The smile faded as quickly as it had shown. Cade was very, very realistic.

Hinges squeaked obnoxiously as someone opened the front door and let in the sound of bullwhip-like cracks of hammers striking nail heads. Sporadic pauses were punctuated by supervisors' shouted directives and the crew's answers. Then the door closed, muffling construction sounds that had, in their own unique way, become white noise over the past eleven months.

And every nail driven home brought them one step closer to completion.

The idea they'd be moving on to the next phase, actually opening the Bar C as a dude ranch to paying customers craving an "Old West experience," rattled Cade yet again. Strangers wandering around what had, for so long, been his private sanctuary. Strangers who would spend their vacation riding his horses and learning to be cowboys for a week before returning to their real lives with jobs that paid well and allowed them to live in the suburbs. They'd drive expensive SUVs and enroll their kids in all sorts of activities. Both husbands and wives would work long hours at jobs they hated in order to fund the lifestyle they'd become accustomed to living. To Cade, it was as foreign a way to live as his day-to-day life was to the same folks he'd be catering to.

Sweat dotted his hairline, a bead of moisture trickling down his temple. He swiped at it with frustration. "Suck it up, buttercup. You signed on for this. From money to mayhem, you knew what the end result would be." Cade entered the bright kitchen at the same time his stomach let out a sonorous rumble.

"You miss breakfast?" Eli asked, moving into the galley from the opposite doorway—he must have been the one who opened the front door. It didn't escape Cade's notice his brother had been reduced to socked feet, as well.

Cade pulled the fridge door open. "Got an early start this morning and wasn't at a place I could stop when the breakfast bell rang." Moving contents around, he grinned when several plastic containers of individually portioned enchiladas came into view. A glance over his shoulder revealed a sheepish grin on Eli's face. "If I didn't know better, I'd believe someone tried to hide these."

"No idea what you're talking about."

"Liar." Cade pulled out two servings and tossed them into the microwave, shut the door and hit Reheat. He faced his brother and leaned his hip against the worn Formica countertop. "Before you go thinking I'm being generous, both of these are mine. Course, I ought to take yours from the fridge as well, just because you're such a selfish old man, hoarding the cook's goods."

Eli's brows drew down in a mock scowl. "Hey. She's *my* woman. You and Ty may benefit from it, but technically she's cooking for *me*."

Cade burst out laughing, fighting to regain control before he answered. "Man, I *dare* you to tell her she 'belongs' to you. Or, even better, tell her she's cooking *for* you. Go on. You might even tell her what she should fix for dinner tonight or that you hate the fabric softener she uses. I'll stand near the phone in case someone has to call in the paramedics, Life Flight or, you know, the National Guard."

Eli's grimace was exaggerated but probably appropriate all the same. "Yeah. I'm not about to say any of those things. Woman's wicked with a blade and a crack shot. She'd probably shoot me in the ass only to 'volunteer' to remove the slug without any kind of numbing agent."

"No, I'd probably shoot you both in the ass and let the wounds fester before I removed the slugs," a feminine voice answered. The woman under discussion strolled into the kitchen, long hair swinging from her high ponytail. Reagan moved straight into Eli's embrace, their lips touching briefly, then lingering over the kiss.

Cade's chest tightened. He'd never dated much, hadn't considered it a priority, and now he couldn't help but wonder what it would be like to have the kind of intense intimacy Eli and Reagan had, the kind that would survive life's fiery trials and rise from tribulation's ashes stronger and surer. Nothing could tear these two apart now.

It didn't bother him that they'd reconnected after Eli found his way home. What ate at Cade was his personal reaction to their undisguised, unguarded happiness. That kind of thing—love, he supposed, if he had to name it—didn't fit anywhere in his life's plans. It never had. Had he been wrong to take that path?

The microwave beeped, and Cade shook off the melancholy before retrieving the leftovers. Hot plastic burned his fingertips, forcing him to juggle the bowls. He tossed them on the counter before grabbing a fork and paper towel. He pulled the lid off the nearest container, forked up a large bite of enchilada and shoved it in his mouth. Less than a second later he was reaching for the fridge, intent on grabbing the first cold thing he found. *Milk.* He twisted the cap off and drank straight from the plastic jug, swallowing rapidly but still spilling it down the sides of his face and soaking his shirt.

"Hot?" Eli asked, the laughter in his voice undisguised.

Cade lowered the jug, glaring at his brother. "I won't taste anything for a week."

"Sucks to be microwave challenged."

Blowing through his nose, Cade flipped his brother off even as Reagan closed in on him.

"How bad is it?" she demanded, wrapping a hand around his neck and pulling him down so she could examine his mouth and throat.

"Not that bad." He pulled against her grip, but she refused to let go.

"Let me see, Cade. No reason to fight me on this if you're sure it's nothing."

Cade closed his eyes and shook his head. "I'm fine, Reagan."

"I'll be the judge of that."

He extricated himself, stepping away. "I burned my mouth, but my brain's only singed. It'll be fine. I'll just finish up and get to work."

She tucked her thumbs in her jeans' pockets. "Whatever suits you."

Eyeing her warily, Cade forked up another bite but blew on it for a good bit before sticking it in his mouth. "Like I said, that would be getting back to work," he said around the food.

Eli pulled Reagan into his arms again, settling her against his chest. "What's on your schedule this afternoon?"

Cade shoveled the food in faster.

"It's not so much this afternoon as it is the next couple of weeks that'll be hell. Got news this morning the interior decorators won't be here with their semi-truck load of furniture until the day before our first guests arrive. Means we'll all have to pitch in to assemble what isn't already put together. Then we'll have to get the rooms set up, beds made, that kind of stuff."

Reagan's eyes widened slightly. "That's cutting it pretty close."

"There's absolutely no room for error, but there's no other option," he muttered around his last mouthful of lunch. "Can't make them get here any faster. I tried." He tossed the container and fork into the sink, the loud clatter startling in the heavy silence.

Reagan stepped out of Eli's arms and began rinsing the dishes and putting them in the dishwasher. "We're having a group lesson on loading the dishwasher soon."

Cade grimaced. "Sorry."

She waved him off. "I actually came in because I wanted to follow up with you guys on the invitations I sent out for the inaugural cattle drive. Anyone have the head count as of today's mail run? I haven't heard from the PR company since Friday. I swear, we need to invest in better internet service. We could've handled all this so much faster than with rural post."

"It's Sunday. Mail doesn't run," Cade offered.

"You know it's bad when you don't even realize what day it is anymore," Reagan grumbled.

Eli moved toward the small built-in desk. "Paper invitations are more personal. That's what Michael Anderson, our contact from the public relations firm, advised, and we're paying a pretty penny for his professional opinion. Regardless, I can give you the head count as of last night." He pulled a worn Day-Timer his way. Absently flipping through several pages, he stopped and did a quick tally. "We have confirmations from twelve of the fifteen, and one regret. Leaves us waiting for the last two responses."

Cade rolled his shoulders. Eli had won the argument about hiring a PR firm. Cade wasn't sure why they'd paid the company so much money to put together a freaking guest list, but he'd given up the argument, keeping his mouth shut about that at this point. "Hard to believe that the moment all those folks show up, the Bar C won't exist anymore."

"She will," Eli countered fiercely. "She *always* will. She's ours." He dropped his head to his chest. They stood in the ensuing silence, each of them surely lost to their own thoughts. Then his chin snapped up. "It's like introducing her with a pseudonym for publicity purposes. She deserved something catchy, and Lassos & Latigos Dude Ranch is perfect for those who haven't met her yet."

Closing his eyes, Cade let his head fall back. "I *still* can't believe you guys took me seriously on that name. I was joking."

"It *is* sort of catchy." The smile in Reagan's voice rang clear.

"So, about the guests who haven't responded?" Cade asked. "Do we chalk them off or plan on them showing up unannounced on opening—"

The phone rang, the jangle of the old bell ringer loud enough to nearly knock Cade out of his socks.

Reagan jerked her chin toward the phone. "Grab that, would you? My hands are wet and Eli's lost in the guest list again. Could be a verbal RSVP."

He hesitated, the idea of talking to a "guest" somewhat daunting.

Then he yanked the phone's receiver off the wall.

"HELLO?"

The gruff voice infused that one word, an alleged greeting, with undisguised caution, throwing Emmaline Graystone off guard. "Hello?"

In the background, dishes clattered in a sink.

Did Michael give me the wrong number? Emma glanced at the invitation, and then checked the display on her smartphone. Nope. Right number.

Her business partner had handled this account save for a couple of phone calls she'd taken in his absence. For those, she'd talked to a man named Eli. He'd been cultured, polished and incredibly professional. This was clearly not the same man.

"Hello?" that deep male voice repeated, his impatience impossible to misinterpret.

"Hello...hi. Um, I'm..." She blew out a soft breath and squared her shoulders. "This is Emmaline Graystone. I'm with Top Priority Publicity, the public relations firm hired by Lassos & Latigos to guide the ranch through it's inaugural—"

"I'm well aware of what your firm has been hired to do, Ms. Graystone. But I was under the impression Eli had been dealing with a man by the name of Michael Anderson."

"Michael is the firm's vice president and has been handling the account, yes. But he's involved in another project where the opening date was unexpectedly moved up and has left him pressed for time. With your grand opening quickly approaching, I offered to take over your account."

"You familiar with our account?" The Voice asked.

She lifted her chin a fraction and stared at the barren horizon. "I'm the firm's president and owner. I've been through your account files extensively, and I fully understand the direction Michael had been taking things. He's done a good job. I can take it from here."

"Glad to hear it."

The perceptible smile in The Voice's response irked her. "Do you have a problem with me assuming this account?"

"Nope. As long as you keep in mind the same principles we drilled into Michael, I don't care who handles our account."

Curious. She hadn't seen anything in the notes about hardline principles to respect. "Which principles, precisely, are you referring to?"

"We want to keep the ranch family focused, make sure it doesn't become a commercial machine but rather an intimate experience for each guest and every booking. Do that and I don't care what kind of equipment's parked behind your zipper."

She blinked wide eyes. "Glad to hear it," she said, mimicking The Voice's dry tone. If this guy was a Covington, and if he would be interacting with ranch guests, they were all in trouble. He couldn't speak to strangers—*paying* strangers—this way.

"You want to talk to Eli?"

"Not necessary. I'm currently standing in the Amarillo airport and there are no rental cars to be had. I would appreciate it if you'd have someone pick me up."

"You're here," The Voice deadpanned.

"If by 'here' you mean at the airport, then yes," she answered, irritated that The Voice offered no courtesy. "More specifically, in case you missed it, said airport is in Amarillo. That would be Texas. Right inside the infamous Panhandle. I'm staring out the huge glass windows at a landscape that's flat, dust-colored as far as the eye can see, and the wind is blowing. It isn't even remotely similar to the brochure Michael created. Still, if that's what you're referring to as 'here,' then the answer stands."

"I should have asked, '*Why* are you here?'" he clarified.

"Unannounced visit to put you through your paces before your guests arrive." She tried not to fume at his ensuing curse. "We have fourteen days to work out any last-minute issues."

He sighed. Something—a hand?—slid over the receiver on the opposite end. The Voice entered into a brief, muffled discussion with what sounded like another man and a woman. The Voice's words, though indiscernible, conveyed his frustration loud and clear. If the dude ranch intended to operate this way, they wouldn't last a single tourist season.

The Voice's hand must have slipped from the receiver

because Emmaline was able to determine the three were arguing over who would drive in to retrieve her. Travelers, particularly those with both the money for the experience and those bringing children, wouldn't tolerate being abandoned at tiny airports as their well-paid "hosts" argued heatedly over who was supposed to have been at the airport to pick them up.

She'd have to put an end to this and figure it out on her own. "Excuse me?"

Nothing. No response whatsoever.

"Excuse me," she said again, louder.

Still no response.

"Hey!" she shouted, ignoring the startled glances from the few passersby in the tiny airport.

"Give me a minute," The Voice ordered.

She ran her fingers through her pixie cut, well aware it would make the ends stand up and not caring one whit. "I've given you more than forty-five between landing and now. If I were an actual customer, I'd be watching the clock, too. Now you're telling me, not asking me, to give you more time. Not the best foot to start out on."

"You're here unannounced, so cut me a little slack." His words were short and sharp.

"I am, yes. And I won't, no," she snapped. "You have one chance to make a first impression. So far? You've blown it. Badly. You'll have to do better with your paying customers or you're finished before you get started."

Silence traveled between them, weaving together to form palpably fractious tension. This was far from the first instance she'd had to assert herself as a woman in a male-dominant world, and if The Voice believed he could wait her out, he had another think coming.

Several minutes passed, the only sound between them their mutual breathing.

The man in the background muttered something and The Voice sighed again, covered the mouthpiece and responded. Then he returned, his breathing soft and steady.

Enough was enough. She'd simply explain to the nameless man that he'd failed her test. She'd send Eli suggestions to fix the problems, namely to find an exceptional surgeon to perform an emergency personality transplant on The Voice. She'd wager everyone would benefit from it.

Leaving would also get her out of covering for Michael on an account where she was personally, uncharacteristically, out of her depth. He had briefed her on the dude ranch before she caught her flight to No Man's Land, but he hadn't mentioned what an incredibly tight-knit family the Covingtons were. She'd picked that up based on correspondence and notes she'd read on the flight into Amarillo. Everything in the file indicated the importance the family had placed—and The Voice had reemphasized—in keeping the ranch an intimate experience, not a commercial Wild West attraction.

Emma knew nothing about families, or how to foster intimacy in any way. A revolving staff of nannies and housekeepers had raised her, faces changing with predictable regularity. No one was ever good enough for her mother, efficient enough for her father or around long enough for the child Emma had been.

That left adult Emma entirely out of her element when it came to family units like the Covingtons. What they had was what she'd coveted all her life, and she had no more idea how to preserve it than she had to fit into it.

That decided it. She'd grab the next flight out of this dustbowl and return to Manhattan. Besides, skipping the dude ranch's inaugural goat roasting or greased pig wrestling or whatever it was wouldn't be a hardship.

She opened her mouth to bow out at the same moment The Voice spoke.

"I'm sincerely sorry for the inconvenience." He paused, clearly out of his element when it came to apologies. "The trip to Amarillo is almost three hours from here. If you'd like to catch a cab to a restaurant, I can pick you up there. Or, if you'd prefer to get a hotel and have a staff member pick you up tomorrow, the ranch will gladly reimburse any expenses you incur. Whatever makes you most comfortable is fine with us, Ms. Graystone."

"It'll take you three hours to get here?"

He cleared his throat. "Yes, ma'am."

"It's early enough in the day to have you come get me at the airport, but—"

"Can I call you back in a second?" The Voice interrupted.

"Sure." Emmaline dropped into a chair at baggage claim. "My cell should be on your caller ID."

"We don't have caller ID out here unless we use our cell or SAT phones. What's your number?"

She rattled it off.

Paper tore. "Gimme a minute." He disconnected before she could respond.

She thumbed her phone off and buried her face in her hands. This wasn't the vision she'd had when she agreed to fill in for Michael. Not even close.

She'd intended to swoop in, wow her country clients, gain a solid recommendation from a new business she believed would be highly successful and disappear immediately after the inaugural event. The high-profile clients they'd invited to the event would get a chance to see her in action, get to know her just a little. Business would pick up again. Things would turn around.

She'd figure out why the firm's profit and loss statement looked as if it was bleeding out for the first time ever. She'd fix it. She'd hire a forensic accountant to examine her books for fraudulent activity. She'd be able to trust Michael again when the P&L was verified, when her suspicions were proven erroneous. She wouldn't doubt his professed loyalty or the fact he was now out of the office more than he was in. All of these things would be resolved. She'd be able to breathe again, to reclaim control of the company and buy Michael out if she had to.

All of which meant she had to stay and somehow make things work with the Covingtons. She was swallowing a prescription antacid when the phone rang. Choking, she bumped Accept and the call connected. Eyes watering, she wheezed out something that resembled, "Emma."

The Voice was there. "You okay, Ms. Graystone?"

"Stellar," she rasped through the next round of harsh coughing.

He waited her out, then said, "I'm going to drive in and pick you up."

Her brows winged up. "You? You're coming to get me yourself?"

He ignored her untempered surprise. "If I leave now, we'll be at the ranch in time for dinner." Clothing rustled in the background, and what sounded like first one and then another heavy shoe thumped against the floor. "Where do you want me to pick you up?"

Emma glanced around as she fought to recover her bearings. "The airport has Wi-Fi, so I suppose here's as easy as anywhere."

"I'll call when I'm five minutes out and you can meet me outside with your gear."

Before she could ask for his cell number in case she

changed her mind and sought out a restaurant, he'd disconnected. Again.

"Great," she answered, anyway. "Can't wait to meet you."

Grabbing her bags, she made her way to one of the small cafés and settled into a booth before pulling her laptop out. She had three hours to kill. Might as well make them productive.

2

CADE HAD BEEN unanimously volunteered for the trip to Amarillo. His protests hadn't made a bit of difference. Eli had argued as only a lawyer could, defending his ability to manage the contractors and keep them lined out. Reagan's efforts were split between working with the installers on the placement of the commercial kitchen appliances in the new dining hall and assisting Tyson, whose favorite, and most valuable, mare had gone into labor.

The animal had been in hard labor for about an hour before Cade left, and Ty wasn't about to let something as mundane a surprise visit from some public relations exec pull him from her side. Reagan might be an entirely capable large animal vet, but the horses were Ty's life. He was there for every major event, beginning with their birth and ending with either their sale or their death.

Singing along with the radio, cruise set on seventy-five and air conditioner blowing hard to combat the afternoon heat, Cade adjusted his rearview mirror to keep the slowly sinking afternoon sun from blinding him. He crested a slight hill, and Amarillo spread out before him. The city sat ensconced beneath a gritty haze, the dust driven by winds he'd guess were easily thirty miles per hour and gusting higher. While there wasn't much in the way of a traditional city skyline, the view still left him with the impression of people surrounding him on all sides. Compared to Roy, the tiny town closest to the ranch, he supposed it was more reality, less impression. Harding County, New Mexico, had a total population of less than seven hundred. Last he'd heard, Amarillo was pushing two hundred thousand residents.

He exited the interstate and took Highway 60 north to Airport Road. Despite wearing sunglasses, he still squinted in the bright light as he pulled out his cell and dialed Ms. Graystone's number.

She answered on the third ring. "Emmaline Graystone."

Her voice, now more cultivated than irritated, was sultry enough he couldn't help but take notice. It warmed a body from the inside out, same as a good whiskey sipped on a cold night.

A small, internal voice reminded him that even the smoothest liquors could deliver a vicious bite. Worse, if a man let the drink go to his head, that same warmth could make him do things he'd regret come morning. Still, Cade couldn't help but wonder how that rich voice would sound in the dark. It wasn't hard to imagine her whispering against his skin, the whisper of her breath hot and moist over bared skin. To consider how she might—

"Hello?"

Cade shifted in the driver's seat, irritably adjusting his fly and trying to stop the path his out-of-control imagination had barreled down. The last thing he needed was to get caught up in a fantasy about an unknown woman's voice—a *contractor's* voice, no less. That particular realization did little to cool the inexplicable lust flooding his system, but it was more than sufficient to clear his mind. "Hi."

"Is…everything okay?" she asked, curiosity unchecked.

"Fine." He cleared his throat. "This is Cade Covington. We spoke earlier when you called the ranch. The dude ranch. Lassos & Latigos." He set the phone face down on his thigh and shook his head. *Just how many dude ranches do you think she called from the Amarillo airport, idiot?* He refocused before replacing the phone to his ear. "I'll be in front of the airport in about five minutes. You want to meet me curbside, or should I come in and get your bags?"

"I'll meet you outside."

"Fair enough. What should I be watching for?"

"I'm about five foot nine, very short dark red hair that's natural and highlights that aren't, black sunglasses, sleeveless black dress. Luggage—two pieces—is also black. I have my messenger bag over my shoulder. You can guess the color. I'm a travel cliché and a pretty drab one at that—everything's black." Her heels clicked across the tiled floor as she began to walk. "My purse is bright red, though. That might help you pick me out of the crush of people."

Her dry humor made him chuckle. "I take it you're used to busier airports than our humble little Amarillo hub."

"I've travelled the world over more than once, Mr. Covington. But an airport with six terminals where at least a dozen men volunteered to retrieve my luggage out of courtesy is a phenomenon I can't even begin to make sense of. I suppose I sound jaded." She laughed softly. In the background, he heard the sound of the doors whooshing open and then the mix of traffic and wind sweeping across her phone's mic. "I'm at the curb. What are you driving?"

He pulled into the passenger drop-off/pickup lane and opened his mouth to answer, but that was as far as his side of the conversation got. He dropped his phone and it bounced off the rubber floor mat, but he made zero effort to retrieve it.

The woman who'd snared his attention pulled her phone from her ear and stared at it in confusion. She had to be Emmaline Graystone. She'd described herself as "drab" only moments before. *She'd flat-assed lied.*

The short, black dress she wore showcased toned arms, a trim waist and lean legs that, based on the gawking of other drivers, were long enough they should've come with a hazard warning. He'd never been a fan of short hair on a woman, but the way the sun lit up her red hair, it appeared almost burnished. And she did, indeed, carry a red purse. All of that was delicious. What she'd neglected to mention were the red lips and siren-red stiletto heels that would be the showcase of his totally inappropriate dreams tonight.

She spoke into the phone, glancing around. Her gaze passed over him, and then snapped back, an eerie recognition on her face. Thumbing her phone off, she dropped it in her bag before reaching up and pulling off her sunglasses.

Cade had dealt with beautiful women before. Emmaline Graystone put every one of them to shame. Her beauty was a quiet demand that he stare whether he wanted to or not. No wonder so many men had offered to help her with her luggage.

The thought made him want to growl. And that shocked him into action. He had no business thinking of her that way. As both a contractor and a ranch guest, she wasn't some random woman at a bar angling to gain his attention or take him home for the night. That fast, his mind ran off with ideas of all the ways he'd want her if she *had* come onto him under those circumstances. He'd figure out what made her tick, discover her every desire, particularly the kind that required no clothes and a lot of one-on-one instruction. In the dark. He fought the urge to punch himself in the temple. Instead, he swallowed his pride and retrieved his phone.

Emmaline had already started toward him, and he inched his truck close to the curb before slamming it in Park. He hopped out and jogged around the front to meet her and take her bags, hoisting them into the crew cab's backseat. The large bags took up the whole bench. Then, steeling himself, he faced her.

In heels, she was only a couple inches shorter than him. Her eyes were the palest green with a dark ring around them. Her nose was short and straight. And her lips… Those lips had been created specifically to go with the rest of her sultry voice and body.

"Since you've taken my bags and put them in your truck, I'm going to assume you're Cade Covington." She arched a brow, considering him. "That or I'm being abducted in broad daylight and allowing it, which I can't imagine I would."

Cade proffered his hand. "Ms. Graystone." His heart skipped a beat. "Nice to meet you, ma'am."

"Call me Emma. Please." She took his hand in a firm shake. "We'd have gotten off to a far better start if you'd laid on the cowboy drawl and charm when you answered the phone."

He shook her hand in return, but when it would have

been polite to release her, he couldn't make himself do it. Instead, he stood there like an idiot, staring at her through dark shades, memorizing her face as if there would be a quiz later.

Her breath stuttered, her hand tightened and then she pulled.

There was no option but to yield to her unspoken demand that he let go. Man, he didn't want to, though. In fact, he wanted to wrap her in his arms, pull her into the line of his body, to discover the type of perfume she wore—and the brand of lingerie.

It was ridiculous in the extreme. Never had a woman affected him this way, and it left his mind entirely scattered. Opening her door, he handed her into the cab without a word and pulled her seat belt forward, settling the clip in her palm.

"Thank you," she murmured as she crossed tanned bare legs that ended in those siren's heels, the dichotomy of elegance and sheer wickedness not lost on him.

No, sir.

This was going to be longest trip to the ranch he'd made from anywhere.

Ever.

EMMA WASN'T SURE what to make of the man in the driver's seat. He'd introduced himself, the deep timbre of his voice stealing the common courtesy of her response before it was halfway out. She wanted to listen to him talk. Didn't matter what he said so long as that voice continued to fill the air around her.

A fine shiver raced over her skin.

That led her straight down the road to considering the way his brief touch had been electrifying, sending little shocks of awareness along her skin. Sure, the contact had been innocent. Her physical response? Not so much. When he'd held on to her, something inexplicable and almost electric had coursed through her. Then she'd tugged, privately engaged in an internal struggle between want and need. She'd desperately *wanted* him to hold on, to maintain the connection between them; she'd *needed* him to let go so she could get her bearings.

But the small gesture had left her craving more skin-to-skin contact, and by "more," her mind was clearly envisioning fewer clothes. Inappropriate images had filled her brain—and that's when her sanity abandoned her, leaving sparse breadcrumbs should she attempt to find her way back to it. There weren't enough to follow, though. Not really. Even if she'd wanted to try. For the record? She hadn't.

In the strangest way, she'd found herself anticipating their road trip. The time in the truck would give her a chance to discover more about both the man and the dude ranch.

Instead of launching into conversation, though, he'd silently put the truck in Drive and pulled away from the curb. That hadn't set well with her, not as her mind raced over all the things she wanted to figure out about him.

Michael's point of contact had been Eli Covington, Cade's brother. Michael had made copious notes about the family's desires for their new business venture, as well as on Eli's experience in corporate law and his wife's role as the ranch's vet. But he'd included very little information on the two other brothers, save that Cade was the middle brother and Tyson the youngest. It would be up to her to fill in the blanks, not only to satisfy her curiosity but to afford her every opportunity to ensure she delivered a service the Covingtons would be satis-

fied with and be willing to broadly recommend. This
trip provided the perfect starting point.

They left the airport via a two-lane highway. A glance
out the window showed flat expanses of desert with occasional arroyos and ever-present, never-ending barbed
wire fences that ran parallel to the highway only to be
swallowed by the distant horizon. Cows were scattered
far and wide. Some fields appeared vacant save for the
intermittent pump jacks that pulled oil from Texas's sub-
terranean depths and sent it on to refineries' holding
tanks. The wind blew hard enough to push the pickup
around a bit, sand peppering the windows like invisible
bullets. Cade never faltered, was never forced to steady
the truck with a second hand. No, he just left his right
wrist draped over the top of the wheel and hid behind
those dark glasses.

What color are his eyes?

The thought caught Emma off guard, all the more so
when she blurted it out.

Cade's brows winged down and mimicked the corners of his mouth. "My eyes?"

Heat skated across her cheeks. "That's apparently how
I decided to break the silence, yes," she muttered.

His lips twitched, but he didn't say anything. Just
stared wordlessly down the long road in front of them
until she was sure she wasn't going to get an answer.

Then he reached up, pushed the brim of his black
Stetson up and slowly pulled his sunglasses off, shifting slightly to face her.

Her breath caught.

"They're just blue."

Definitely blue, but far, far from "just." His medium
brown hair and the darkening hint of what would become a five-o'clock shadow made his eyes appear the

pale color of sunlight caught in arctic ice. A much deeper blue ringed the iris. Combined, the two colors created a startling contrast.

Cade rolled his shoulders before shoving his sunglasses on again. "They're blue," he said gruffly.

"And Ballyportry Castle could be called stacked stone. Oversimplifying it doesn't make it any less impressive," she bit out, both embarrassed and irritated.

His lips twitched again. "You comparing my eyes to some stone castle?"

"No." She settled deeper into the captain's chair. "Stone's cold and gray, not blue."

"Then why bring up...what was it? Bally-something?" At her silence, he shot her a quick glance. "Emma?"

The sound of her name on his lips made her stomach roll over like a lazy hound lying under the summer sun. "Ballyportry. And I brought it up because I was just there. It's in Ireland. The place made an impression. For better or worse, so do you. The difference is that the impression *you* make is more frustrating than fascinating." She kicked off her heels and tucked one foot under her. No better time than now to begin filling in those blanks. "How in the world did you ever end up winning your wife over?" she groused.

"I'm not married." Amusement made the corners of his eyes crinkle when he smiled. "So, I make an impression, do I?"

"Girlfriend?" she asked.

"No wife, no girlfriend and no friend with benefits." His gaze shifted to her then returned to the road where late-afternoon heat was stirring up thunderheads on the horizon. "I'd rather talk about this impression I make."

"First impression was on the phone. You and the castle are the same there—generally unwelcoming." His smile slipped, but she pressed on. "On meeting, it's clear both you and the castle are immovable. Now, traveling through what seems to be an almost alien landscape, it's clear you each situate yourself in the midst of an irascible environment. And if the castle could express emotion, I'd say you both enjoy the fact that the majority of the visitors to your little corner of the world don't speak the native language."

He pulled off his sunglasses and tossed them on the dash again before cutting her a sharp look. "Almost sounds as if you don't think much of me."

"I don't *know* you, and after spending a couple of weeks with you, I doubt I'll either fall madly in love with you or run screaming from the sheer terror of ranch life. I'd quite prefer it if you'd tell me a little something about yourself, Mr. Covington." He harrumphed, and one corner of her mouth curled up. "I'll concede here…Cade."

"Concede, is it?"

"Seems appropriate since this has evolved into a verbal joust." A grin spread across her face, surprising her. The verbal sparring was actually fun. She found she enjoyed pricking his ego a bit, so she pressed on. "I don't suppose cowboys joust, do they? Might be a fun diversion for guests at the dude ranch."

He scowled, hands twisting the leather-wrapped steering wheel until it squeaked in protest. "Look. I ride. I rope. I wrangle. I do *not* freaking *joust*. And, above all, I should never be mistaken for some knight in shining armor. And before you ask, that also means I don't have or want a damsel in distress. Clear enough?"

Emma pursed her lips and shifted to her hip to consider him full on. "Odd. I was under the impression cowboys were all about saving the day."

"You've watched too much TV, Emma." He retrieved his sunglasses and slid them on his face with practiced calm.

"Fair enough. If I'm not up to speed on the way cowboys really behave or what they seem to want, educate me."

He choked, color climbing up from under the collar of his shirt and rising until it reached the band of his hat and disappeared. "Educate you? What do you want to know?" The skepticism in his voice made her laugh out loud. This was so much fun she'd have to add "baiting Cade Covington" to her list of hobbies.

Untucking her foot, she crossed her legs.

Cade's eyes glazed over and the rough-around-the-edges cowboy was forced to overcorrect to get the truck back on the road.

She crossed her hands in her lap, the picture of innocence. "Educate me the cowboy way, I suppose."

Cade slowed the truck and pulled it to the side of the empty road. He threw one arm around the headrest of her seat and shifted on his hip to face her. "You want an education?"

The undisguised, unapologetic heat in his voice paired with the sharp smell of rain and ozone from the brewing storm and caused her heart to race to a tattooing beat inside her chest.

"I don't believe I stuttered," she managed to get out without her voice shaking.

He traced the line of her jaw, his touch as heated as a branding iron. "This ought to be interesting, then. Want to wager on the results?"

"What?"

"You'll end up loving or loathing me, darlin'. Which will it be?"

Caught up in the intensity of his pale blue stare, she stuttered. "L-love or loathing?"

"That's right, Ms. Graystone," he replied softly, pushing his black Stetson up, again revealing those just-blue eyes. "You're stuck with me for the next two weeks by your own doing…Emma. So what do you want to bet you either love me or loathe me by the time it's all over?"

Her wits had become veritable marbles rolling around all willy-nilly inside her. She mentally gathered what she could, forced herself to slow down and then smiled with enough heat to make the asphalt seem frosty. "You want to play? Then we'll play. But there have to be mutually agreeable, and equally impressive, stakes."

Now it was Cade who, licking his lips, only nodded.

"If I leave here loathing you, you'll donate a week at the ranch to the charity of my choosing."

"And if you end up loving me?" His words were strained, voice so dry it was almost dusty.

"'Love' is a little strong, don't you think? That emotion requires time to grow and prosper, and two weeks won't cut it."

His eyes heated. "Ever been in love, Emma?"

Warmth suffused her cheeks. "Not really a believer in happily-ever-after endings."

"No? What do you believe in, then?"

She shrugged.

"C'mon, Emma. There has to be something," Cade pressed. "And why *wouldn't* you believe in true love?"

"You can't believe in something you've never seen, never experienced."

His eyes widened. "Yeah, actually, you can. It's called having faith in someone or something. It's like sitting down in a chair. I know it's a chair because, even if I personally have never sat in a chair, I've watched others do it. So when I go to sit down, I have faith the chair will do what it was supposed to do and hold me up because I've witnessed it do so for others. Faith." He reached up and undid the collar button on his shirt. "You probably understand more about love than you realize you do, Emma. You've witnessed it, whether over dinner with friends or between a man and woman standing on a busy street corner, so caught up in each other they miss their bus and don't care. That's love, so you've got something to draw on."

She shifted in her seat, her gaze roaming the grandeur of the plains, her mind trying to commit the smallest details to memories.

He pressed further. "So, what—you want me to believe you've never loved anyone and never seen someone in love?" He settled his black Stetson firmly before shaking his head. "I don't buy it, Ms. Graystone. Someone who looks like you? She's been loved before, even if from afar."

"It's pretty to think so, isn't it? Regardless, appearances have no bearing on love, particularly true love. Have you never watched a Disney movie? *Beauty and the Beast*, for example. Beautiful woman falls in love with a man cursed to beastly form. But love changes everything, making her whole and him the handsome prince he'd been before." Emma fought to keep the bitterness out of her voice. "A fantastic tale that creates false hope in girls." She choked on a bitter laugh. "As a kid, I wasn't given anything but the hard truth. No disillusionment. Ever."

"My old man was a real piece of work, too. Mom? We all swore she was an angel, but we lost her way too early. I get the maladjusted family bit," he said, resting his wrist across the steering wheel casually. "We've all got some kind of dysfunction that dogs our heels. Doesn't mean we have to let it herd us where it will, though."

"You think I let my history determine my future?" *How could he judge her?* "I grew up with nannies. Some were young and nubile and spent a great deal of time in my father's office. Then there were the rigid hardliners who stayed just long enough to offend my mother before being dismissed.

"It didn't matter which camp they were in, though. Affection was forbidden. They were there to raise me, not coddle me." She forced a smile. "My parents hated each other, but it was a strategic financial match, a practical investment of individual strengths in order to achieve mutual goals. So tell, me, Cade. Where in all of that should I have found faith in love and family? Perhaps somewhere between courses at dinner when I was allowed to eat with my parents so long as I didn't speak? Or maybe at school, where my parents were the repeat no-shows for everything from concerts to parent-teacher conferences? No? I've got it! How about when I thought I'd bank on love and entered into a joint business venture they approved of with a man they'd chosen and suggested I marry in order to forge a stronger connection between the family businesses?" Her mind flashed to Michael, her business partner, the same one she currently suspected might be sabotaging the business she'd started before she'd met him and allowed him to buy in. "You'll have to forgive me if I don't get totally on board with the whole 'love saves the day' mentality."

Lines appeared at the corners of Cade's mouth as his frown deepened, but he didn't comment on her outburst. He simply drove on, only the radio and road noise cutting the silence.

The reference to Michael reminded Emma of her worries. She'd left him a voice mail this morning, asking him to call her as soon as possible. The only thing she'd received was a text. "Good luck in the Wild West, Annie Oakley! Send a picture of you on a horse. Thanks for taking over this account and assuming responsibility for the Covington's new dude ranch."

The last line had bothered her. Why had he laid responsibility for both the account and, in particular, his clients at her feet?

"I'm under no delusions about what I want," Cade said. His words sounded louder in a truck cab that had been silent as they'd traveled across the flat grassland all the way to the base of a mountain range.

She shook off thoughts of Michael. "Want? For what?"

"For our wager. When I have you wrapped around my little finger with love in your eyes, I want you to refund the money we've paid you and do all the PR and marketing for the dude ranch pro bono for the next two years."

"I'll take those stakes." And she would do it without regret. There was a better chance of her taking up competitive hurling—Ireland's official "sport" that was more like sanctioned war with blunt objects and no armor— than fall in love.

She glanced at him to gauge his reaction and found herself nearly struck dumb by the unguarded thrill of challenge on his face. One corner of Cade's mouth kicked up to reveal a deep dimple, then he winked at her. He shifted his attention to the long stretch of road before them that appeared, from her vantage point, as if it turned into the mountain and then was swallowed by it.

He'd *winked* at her.

There'd been nothing offensive at all in the flirtatious

gesture, but her body's response was positively traitorous. Heat bloomed between her thighs. She rubbed her legs together subtly, longing for his touch, absolutely craving the kind of heat a man like Cade could offer, the kind that would assuage her unanticipated, uncomplicated desires. Her heart beat a rock-hard rhythm inside her chest and a fine sweat decorated her upper lip.

Images of the two of them intertwined flashed through her brain. Her imagination had *definitely* missed the memo that she was a woman who did not have physical or emotional responses. But, client or not, she craved Cade's touch like a hummingbird craved nectar—in a mandatory, had-to-have-it kind of way.

Forcing her attention to the quickly changing scenery, she watched as they traversed a bridge straddling a wide but shallow and very rocky creek.

She also noticed that the blue of the sky was slowly being eaten away by encroaching dark clouds that were tinged with the oddest shade of green. Gesturing to the clouds, she found her voice. "Is that going to be okay?"

Cade glanced at her. "You're safe with me, Emma."

She nodded and swallowed so loud he had to have heard it over the radio. "Sure." Unbidden, a quote from Mark Twain wandered through her consciousness. The famous wordsmith had said, "There is a charm about the forbidden that makes it absolutely desirable." And he'd been absolutely right.

She'd never been sexually attracted, let alone *tempted*, by a client. Cade had broken that track record. Shattered it, really. But he'd broken Twain's theoretical "rule." Cade had *started out* desirable—the kind of desirable that made a woman throw caution to the wind and go where chance led her. Whatever this thing was, she'd negotiate with regret later. For the first time, Emma wanted to set all the pressures of life and work aside and do nothing more than simply experience what it was to be alive.

She knew with inexplicable certainty that this man could give her that.

3

THE REST OF the trip back to the ranch could only be compared to jockeying a Shetland pony in the Kentucky Derby: a bumpy ride that seemed it would never end. The heat between them refused to dissipate no matter how high Cade ran the air-conditioning. She kept shooting him covert glances from the corners of her eyes. He knew because he was caught up doing the same thing, thereby catching the majority of interest in those brilliant green eyes.

What the hell am I playing at?

He was a cowboy—he didn't understand the type of sexual byplay that involved a high-powered, corporate woman who'd walk in and out of his life so fast she'd leave his head spinning. The woman probably collected men the way most women around here collected canning jars. Store them on the shelf until she had a use for them and put them away when that usefulness passed. Cade would never allow himself to be put on a shelf any more than he would live through the daily wear and tear a relationship would bring. And what in God's name was he doing, thinking in terms of jam jars and relationships? He'd only met Emma three hours ago. Yeah, they'd flirted, but that didn't mean he'd be off ring shopping come morning.

The last sliver of sun disappeared behind the variable peaks and crags of the Sangre de Cristo Mountains, casting the early-evening sky in broad swaths of brilliant color. The storm brewed southwest of them, spitting lightning as the winds increased and kicked up dust.

He pulled off his sunglasses and clipped them to the visor. At the rate the two of them were going, he and Emma would make it to the ranch before full dark set in roughly an hour from now. When Eli, the attorney in the family, heard how the trip had gone down, when he learned that Cade had flirted with and challenged a contractor-slash-guest about falling in love, the fact that they were blood wouldn't keep Cade's ass out of the sling his older brother would aim to park it in. The only blood that *would* matter was whatever they shed as they beat the crap out of each other. Most annoying? Cade knew he had it coming. Every. Meaty. Fist.

His grip on the steering wheel tightened until he was choking the ever-loving hell out of the black leather. Sometime in the past half hour, the radio had officially devolved to short bursts of music followed by long runs of staticky white noise. The sound skipped across his nerves like a stone across water. Every point of contact was brief but annoyingly sharp.

If the dude ranch did well, the first thing he'd invest in was satellite radio. Screw the recurring expense. They could use it to play music in the sawdust-floored dining hall during gatherings and events. Hell, if he was going off the deep end anyway, maybe he'd forgo his cautious nature altogether and order the setup when he got home. He'd even add a second receiver to his truck as a personal bonus.

Mind on the possibilities of satellite radio, Cade reached out and turned down the volume, switching the output from FM to CD. Tyler Farr's voice poured out of the sound system, his mournful song telling a story of heartbreak and betrayal. If Cade's soul could have audibly sighed, it would have. Good music always did that for him, helping him calm and find his center no matter how strung out he was. Years of habit made Cade take a couple of deep breaths. Settling into the music, he began to sing.

Emma rounded on him, eyes wide. With deliberate care, she slipped her sunglasses into her short hair, little strands standing out in every direction. "What are you doing?" she asked.

Cade jerked, twisting the steering wheel to the right as he shot Emma a sharp look. "Singing. Why? Would you rather listen to the static?" He reached for the radio controls, surprised when she gripped his wrist hard enough the smaller bones ground together. Extricating his hand, his reproach was gentle. "That's my roping hand."

"Sorry." Her apology, issued on a single breath, seemed almost anxious. "Will you sing some more?"

His brow creased. "Why?"

"Your voice is…" She waggled one hand between them before flattening it over her heart and drawing a slow, deep breath. "I've never heard anything as striking. Beautiful, even."

Heat burned across his cheeks and he wished the option to hide behind his sunglasses still existed. "I don't usually, uh, sing. For people."

Her eyes widened. "Why on earth not? Your voice is amazing!"

"My mother…" He hesitated.

"She must have been proud," Emma said on a soft smile.

"She died when I was nine. Last request she had was that I sing her to sleep." His eyes burned, piquing both his irritation and his embarrassment. He tried to clear the gruffness from his throat.

She moved forward a fraction, froze, then settled deeper into her seat. "I'm so sorry," she whispered. "I can relate, though. I lost both of my parents at once."

"Accident?"

She nodded. "Two years ago."

"I'm sorry."

"Me, too, but probably not as sorry as you were— are—about your mother." Heat stained her cheeks a deep rose. "Forget I said that. I apologize."

"I'm surprised the fact we lost her so early on didn't make it into the commercial file you have on the ranch."

"Why would it?"

"Just seems it would've been a marketing ploy—three brothers brought together after the loss of their mother but driven in different directions." He shrugged. "Almost seems too easy to avoid using."

"I would *never* exploit your pain that way," she bit out.

"You don't seem the type, maybe, but what about the guy that's been working with Eli? What's his name…" He rubbed his chin. "Michael?"

"Your account's in my hands now. I won't take easy routes or cheap shots."

The invisible fist around his heart eased up some, but he couldn't thank her. Not yet. The most he could manage was, "Good to know."

"I've been working my way through the file. Michael has a lot of notes, so it's taking a bit to sort through it all."

He shot her a hard glance. "Cutting it a little close,

having someone new take over so near the event. You don't—*can't*—possibly understand what we want for the place." *Or, more importantly, what they* didn't *want.*

Emma nodded. "In general, I agree. But what I'm envisioning as we drive is a remoteness that's become a way of life, a sense of total privacy, of communion with your heritage and your responsibilities to earth and animal. Definitely not the big, commercial, circus-y production you find in lower-end travel brochures."

Cade fought the urge to let gravity have its way with his jaw, pulling the damn thing open. *How could she possibly key into the very things that were important to the family? How could she read all of them so well without ever having* met *them?* "Is that what Michael had in his notes?" It was the only explanation.

Grimacing, she shook her head. "He had plans for showy ads and more adventure-style photography. I'll have a lot to do to change directions in two weeks, but it can be done. First thing I'll do tonight is issue, via email, a formal stop order for all advertising until I can provide new directives in writing. I want a paper trail. Then I'll revisit the long-term exposure plans that Michael created for your account."

Shooting her yet another quick glance, he was surprised at the ferocity on her face. "Problems in paradise?"

"While there are undeniable perks, the reality is that owning your own commercial business is far from paradise." Her eyelids fluttered shut, her head thumping the headrest. "Let's leave this conversation with 'I'm looking into it' and fully intend to keep your account on my personal client list."

Hmm. "Dun & Bradstreet didn't give you a bad report by any means, but Eli said your creditworthiness had slipped in the last twenty-four months due to some serious fluctuations in cash flow when compared to the previous five years." The shock on her face said she hadn't expected them to do such intensive research on her.

"If you have concerns regarding my company's financial stability or my ability to do my job—" she started, but Cade cut her off.

"We hired you. That ought to tell you everything you need to know. We're not the type to make poor business decisions." He couldn't stop himself from adding, "We can't afford to."

The next few mile markers passed in silence, the emotional tension escalating inside the truck seeming to rival the storm building outside. Anxiety crackled between them as true as Mother Nature's lightning did between sky and earth. The charge in the air gave off the same general discomfort, the kind that said, "Take cover." Cade tried to reduce the strain by changing the subject.

"I've never been to New York," he offered.

"Hmm." Emma continued to stare out the window.

"You can do better than that, Graystone." So could he. "Tell me something about yourself, seeing as none of us have really talked to you."

"What would you like me to volunteer?" The question was polite but lacked the force of personality she'd shown.

"You single?"

Surprise colored her cheeks and brightened her eyes as she whipped around to face him. "What? That's irrelevant when it comes to our business dealings."

He fought the urge to grin. "Not really. The bet still stands. Love or loathing. No way can I win if you're going home to someone in two weeks, someone who's already got your heart. Of course," he said, openly considering her, "I can't imagine you're the type to take such a wager if you had someone back home. And I doubt you'd have such a...unique take on happy endings if you were working toward your own, would you."

When she didn't answer, he rested his right forearm against the headrest on her seat, letting his fingers trace the silken skin of her neck. He was struck by the urge to move his fingers higher. Following the instinct, he played through the hair at her nape. Soft but thick.

He fought the craving to massage up her neck until he could play with the thick mass over her crown. He should move away, stop touching her, his personal temptation, without remorse. He was about to pull his hand away when she made a slight sound of encouragement. "Feel good?"

"Didn't realize how stressed I've been."

"So, will you answer me?" he said gently, never ceasing his tender attention.

Tipping her chin forward to give him better access, she mumbled, "I did. I said I didn't realize I was so stressed."

"That's not what I was after, Emma, and you know it. Are you involved with anyone?"

She shifted in her seat, forcing Cade to move his hand. His fingertips brushed over the thin skin protecting her life vein. He paused, only briefly, but it was long enough to experience the thunder of her pulse beneath his thumb. He dropped his hand to the console between them. "You're single."

"You can't be sure of that," she objected. "I haven't answered you."

"Don't have to." Had she been seeing anyone, he had this innate, inexplicable knowledge she would never have taken the bet. She wasn't that person. That was answer enough at this point. It also left him with plenty to consider. He cranked the radio up, trying to buy himself time to think.

A gust of wind caught the truck and pushed the behemoth like it was no more than a paper kite in the wind. The storm clouds had taken on a deeper greenish-gray tone that colored the land an odd, pre-twilight color that was impossible to mistake. Mother Nature was advising everyone in the county that she was about to unleash a can of whoop-ass. The wise man would hunker down. Problem was, there was no way Cade could get them to the ranch before the heavens loosed their fury. If it hailed, it could total his truck. Lightning posed the largest threat, though. They'd be okay on the flats if they stayed in the car.

As a rancher, he spared a thought for the poor animals. They didn't always have a way to get out of this kind of mess, and if they balled up in a fence corner, the ranch would lose a few to electrocution when lightning struck the metal fencing.

Emma unbuckled her seat belt, twisted around and half climbed into the backseat.

"What're you doing?"

A gust of wind slammed into the pickup, shoving the big vehicle hard enough it knocked Emma into him. She landed with her hip on his shoulder, that luscious ass in his face. The urge to nip it was nearly too much.

Her muffled reply caught him off guard. "Grabbing my camera."

"Your *camera*?"

Another gust of wind parked her hip over his shoulder. She pushed herself up, clutching a black bag large enough to hold decent digital equipment.

Then she realized the predicament she was in. She

had one knee solidly between his thighs and the other rested against the outside of his right hip. Her breasts were pressed intimately against his chest and arm. Her far hand was digging into his pectoral pad. She dipped her chin and peered down at him, her eyes wide with surprise. "How did I end up in your lap?"

His right hand moved of its own volition, coming to rest on the indention of her waist. "Your camera, Emma."

She swallowed hard and nodded, a couple quick jerks of her chin. "The storm. I wanted a picture of the storm. I've never…"

"Never what?" he asked, urging her to finish her statement.

Without breaking her gaze, she set her camera bag in her seat and wrapped her hand around the nape of his neck. "I've never experienced anything similar to this. Never encountered anything so wild and free, something that acts without consequence or—"

"There're always consequences." His voice had devolved into a gruff whisper. "Always," he repeated, tracing his thumb over her bottom lip.

"I'll live with them," she said, voice husky.

"All of them? Just like that?"

"Every. Single. One."

So be it.

EMMA COULDN'T LOOK AWAY. Cade's voice, sultry and wanting, had wiped out her every effort to maintain her composure. From the moment she'd met him, he'd had her heart rate speeding up in all the right ways. And for the last hundred miles, she'd been crossing and recrossing her legs in an effort to assuage the mild ache in her core. Then he'd sung. Just a few notes. That's all it had taken to push her over sanity's edge.

Driven by madness or not, she couldn't give him complete control. No one held that over her head. Not ever. She would manage the way this happened—and it *would* happen. The undisguised desire on his face, that same face that had been so passive since meeting her, now empowered her. It was the type of desire a woman didn't *want* to discount any more than she would the impressive bulge fighting to destroy his zipper.

She tossed her glasses onto the seat beside her before tipping up the rim of his cowboy hat. Tracing her fingers along the rough stubble lining his jaw, she leaned forward and laid her cheek next to his, her lips against his ear. "Just so I'm completely clear. You're not involved at any level? Because I'll never be anyone's other woman or second choice."

"Not involved, and you're far from my second choice. You're the first woman who's ever crawled under my skin like this," he replied, tension threaded through every word. His grasp on her hip tightened.

"That's a powerful statement." She nipped his ear. "Power is seductive, is it not?"

His breath came out in a rush. "You're playing with fire, darlin'."

She couldn't help but agree any more than she could stop the rush of heat up her neck and down through her belly. This man was sin incarnate, from his boots to his jeans to his very, *very* fine body. Everything about him appealed to her. She'd never experienced this crazy rush of desire, the raw cravings that made her want to accept his stupid challenge and discover just what two weeks might bring. With absolutely no intention of falling in love, she could still enjoy the chase, the seduction, the touching and… She shivered.

Then she smiled, the stubble on Cade's cheek leav-

ing a slight whisker burn on her delicate skin. "I understand exactly what I'm doing, *darlin'*. I may be single,
but I've never been celibate. I take liaisons as more than
a casual fling but less than a plea for serious commitment. Clear?" She pressed closer, her lips brushing the
shell of his ear. "And as for fire? You have no…idea…
just how good it would be to burn with my particular
brand of heat."

Cade silently worked his jaw, the muscles and tendons
in his neck standing out in sharp relief. She'd balanced
herself by placing one hand on his headrest and the other
against his ribs. Beneath the one hand, his heart pounded
out a hard, fast rhythm. And she'd caused it.

Satisfaction rolled through her. It blazed, reducing
any remaining hesitation to ash and clearing the path
for her to touch, to taste, to experience this man who'd
clearly kidnapped her common sense. This so wasn't
her norm. She was adventurous and fun loving, yes.
To do her job, she had to be. But in her private life, she
was far more cautious, always weighing the risks. Because once two people crossed a certain line, there was
no going back. Ever.

"Hold on," Cade snarled before he braked rapidly and
yanked the wheel. Hard.

Emma tightened her thighs around his to keep from
being tossed across his lap. She clutched his shirt in
one hand and wrapped her other arm around his rigid
shoulders, clinging to him and not sorry for the action
or the opportunity.

They hit the dirt road at speed.

A shout of exhilaration escaped her as he wrestled the
fishtailing behemoth into submission before stomping
the accelerator. This, *this* was what she'd been so sure
he could give her. In a lifetime of structure and bound-

aries, she was suddenly living, *alive* in a way she'd never been before.

They flew down a two-track dirt road, kicking up an impressive dust trail. The walls of the canyon rose around them and grew steeper the farther they went. They crossed a cattle guard so fast the truck hardly chattered over the pipes, but Cade still accelerated. Images outside the windows became blurred. But all she could focus on was the fierce, untamed expression that had taken over his entire appearance.

Daylight had abandoned them almost completely. They rounded a curve in the road and, before Emma realized what was happening, Cade left the two-track lane and headed across a wide field. She shifted to watch as the headlights flashed over a huge copse of aspens, their white bark startling in the halogen glare.

Canyon walls closed in tighter around them and drew the eye up, showcasing the building storm. Thunderheads roiled. Lightning flashed, nature's strobe, and thunder rumbled a bass line. The storm would roll over them in minutes, but at the moment? The sliver of deepening night sky that could be seen was filled with brilliant pinpricks of starlight.

Cade rolled down the front windows.

The smell of rain and the charge of electricity in the air filled the cab.

Her last coherent thought fled, leaving nothing but instinct in its wake. She yanked at his shirt to pull him toward her, or her toward him. She wasn't sure. Didn't matter. The hem pulled free and her knuckles brushed down the edge of his abs and into a gutter created by his lats. She'd been relatively certain he was built. Now she had to revise her opinion to acknowledge he was honed and defined in a way that could make a woman's common sense take a vacation while her body enjoyed the fruits of his labor—thick cords of muscle, ridges and valleys of definition, smooth skin interrupted by only the thinnest line of hair from his belly button and disappearing into his pants.

His arm banded around her.

She instinctively tightened her grip on him.

He slammed on the brakes, sliding the truck to a stop amidst the trees. A dust cloud rolled over them, but it was quickly blown away by the storm's volatile winds.

Thunder boomed louder.

Ozone tickled her nose.

Cade shoved open the door and, pulling her into his arms, took her with him when he hopped down from the cab. He carried her with sure steps to the rear of the truck before he set her down.

She wobbled, her heels sinking into the dirt. "My shoes—"

"Stay on," he said, blindly reaching for the tailgate handle and lowering the impromptu seat. Raw need made his smooth voice deeper, giving it a rough, commanding edge. His eyes darkened.

The first drop of rain hit her bare arm. She shivered. "This is crazy." She took a step back and her ass hit the edge of the tailgate.

He reached out and wrapped his hand around her neck, tightening his grip. "Insane."

Emma nodded her head, the movement minute. "There's a zipper on the side. Pull it."

Cade found the zipper tab and hesitated. "Do you want this, Emma? Say no and it all stops."

Her pulse fluttered faster than a hummingbird's wings. "And if I say yes?"

A flash of lightning lit his face, burning his image

into her mind in stark relief before she was left blinking and trying to see through the burnout that had stolen her sight. She reached out and laid a hand flat on Cade's chest.

"This is irresponsible," he said softly.

"Irrational."

"Mad."

She hesitated before offering, "Undeniable."

He moved in, his hard body pressing against her. "Done," he whispered, his mouth closing the distance between them.

The sky opened up the moment he kissed her.

4

FOR A SPLIT SECOND, Cade was certain the cold water
should steam off his skin where it hit. And all due to
a kiss. But this was more than *a* kiss. It was *the* kiss.
It rocked him, sending a heady rush through his body.
They stood there getting lost in each other as the cold
New Mexico rain thoroughly soaked them.

Her lips were full and pliant. Scalding heat radiated
off her body. She opened to him. Her tongue darted out
to taste him in a bold caress. The move, quick and yet
almost questioning, nearly undid him. He groaned, the
sound carried away by the wind that whipped through
the grass and rattled leaves.

He couldn't let the moment go, tasting her with the
same surety as she'd done him. She had the faintest hint
of mint on her tongue. He couldn't remember her having eaten, as if she'd eaten candy at some point. In the
dark, with her wet body sealed against his, she smelled
of clean cotton and the very storm itself. Underneath that
was, he assumed, whatever musky perfume she wore.
The combination all but drove him to his knees.

Warm heat spread through him as their limbs tangled
together, her legs inhibited by the cut and length of her

dress until, with a noise of obvious frustration, she hiked the hem up to her waist.

Cade gripped her under the arms and set her on the tailgate, moving between her thighs when she grabbed his shirt and tugged.

"Off," she murmured against his lips, pulling at the buttons.

He yanked at his shirt, those very buttons scattering in every direction. She helped him peel the denim down his arms, and they jointly flung it free as the cuffs cleared his hands.

Their mouths reconnected frantically. He took the kiss deeper. Or did she? Whatever. The only things that mattered were hands and tongues and teeth, lips and sharp, short sounds of encouragement that trumpeted their own wild intent. Both soft and calloused hands swept over bared skin wherever they found it. Lightning skipped cloud to cloud and the resulting thunder echoed in its wake. But even Mother Nature wasn't strong enough to stop what they'd started.

He'd lost himself in her so fast. Never before had a woman pulled at him like this. Never before had he become a slave to taste, smell, touch or the smooth satin of rain-slicked skin under his work-roughened hands. Never had he expected to find someone with the power to drive him out of his mind. No way did he want to lose this moment—or this woman.

Cade ran his hands up Emma's sides and found the zipper for the dress under her left arm. His fingers seemed too large, too clumsy to deal with the delicate dress. Fumbling with the tab, he cursed.

She pushed at his hand.

His fingers were wrapped in the dress, and he pulled. Fabric ripped.

Struggling, she broke the kiss and glared. "This was my favorite dress."

"I'll buy you another one."

She yanked him into her again, her mouth searing his as she shimmied her upper body free of the garment.

Make that five. I'll buy her five more.

He slid his hands up the sides of her thighs as the storm picked up force. Wind whipped the rain against his skin. Her bare legs had goose bumps. Intent on pulling her into the warmth of the truck, he broke the kiss again and made to move away.

Emma wrapped her legs around his waist and pulled him into her with a bold stare. "Not yet."

"You're cold."

"Not where it matters."

At her admission, her words husky and laden with wicked intent, he had a singular moment where he was afraid he was going to orgasm with no one touching him.

Like hell.

She pulled him tight to her, fumbling with his belt buckle. A sound of unadulterated need escaped her as the denim-clad ridge of his erection slid across the silk of her panties, riding just the right spot.

So he did it again.

Emma writhed even as she wrapped her hands around his neck. Lips against his, she whispered, "Get those pants undone, cowboy."

"Tell me what you want," he demanded, hands first dealing with his belt buckle, and then working his pants and boxer briefs down. His erection sprang free, hard as a cured two-by-four.

The tip of her tongue traced the bow of her upper lip as she looked him over. Then her eyes met his. "All of it." Her gaze dipped and she took a shuddering breath that translated through the most intimate points of contact between them. "I want everything you have to give, Cade."

He fished for his wallet, his waterlogged pants complicating things as they slid down his legs. Finally getting ahold of it, he pulled it free as Emma grabbed his rigid cock, stroking it from tip to root with a firm hand. Cade closed his eyes and raised his face to the sky as his hips surged forward. Unable to stop himself, he shouted as he pumped into her stroking fist.

The burn began at the base of his spine. Gripping her wrist, he pulled her hand away from him and sheathed himself. His breaths came short. "You have to stop before I completely lose it."

All he wanted was to flip her over and drive into her again and again, to lose himself in this woman who brought him to life, who crushed the thick conservative shell he'd erected over the years to subdue his wild side, and who made nothing matter but the moment. She was his next breath, his next heartbeat, the whole of his desire.

She slid off the tailgate and shed the rest of the dress. Standing there in her silk underwear, she asked, "Isn't that the point?" Then she undid her bra and tossed it in the bed of the truck with a wicked grin. "You destroyed my classic Chanel LBD. You're not ruining my La Perla."

"I have no clue what the hell you're talking about, and I don't care." Whatever La Perla was, he'd burn it to the ground if it meant exposing more of her to his hungry gaze. He stared at her breasts. Luscious and full, with dusky nipples that had beaded with cold, or arousal, or both.

Water dripped off the tips of her nipples. He leaned forward and laved one point before suckling the rainwater from her skin.

Emma arched in to him and cried out, knocking his cowboy hat from his head as she threaded her fingers through his hair. Pulling him closer, she encouraged him to switch breasts.

He blindly followed her suggestion, desperate to taste every inch of her skin.

Her fingers tightened in his hair, then tugged. "Cade."

His name, little more than a whimper, drew his gaze to hers.

Eyes wild, Emma crushed her mouth to his, their tongues dueling, tasting, taking.

The result was primal. It was the only explanation he had for his behavior. She provoked that in him, reduced him to the most fundamental and basest of man whose needs overrode common sense and courtesy. He would never hurt her, but he *would* have her.

Now.

EMMA HAD EXPECTED to have a little fun, to fool around, get the sexual tension worked out between them, and then resume the trip to the ranch. She hadn't expected to find this insanely sensual man lurking inside the quiet, composed cowboy she'd met earlier. This man seemed sexually starved, driven by a kind of uninhibited passion she'd never experienced before. And he brought the same out in her. He made her want things she'd never wanted, beginning with the kind of sex she was about to have—in the open, under a storming sky, with a veritable stranger.

She didn't care.

Cade grabbed her hips and spun her around, the heel of one shoe catching against a tuft of grass.

The heel snapped, and Emma stumbled. Strong arms

caught her as a deep, dark voice breathed across her ear. "I won't let you fall."

"But—"

"Trust me," he murmured, nipping the outer edge of her ear. "Kick your bad shoe off and bend over the tailgate."

Strong hands directed her, helping her keep her balance. He stroked one hand slowly down her neck, between her breasts and around the underside of her right breast, continuing down her ribs and coming to rest at her hip. She pushed at him.

With a squeeze, he pressed the hot, hard length of his erection between her butt cheeks. He leaned over her and whispered in her ear, "Still willing to take everything I have to offer, Ms. Graystone? Because we're about to cross a line here, a line we can't come back from."

All she heard was "come," and it's all she wanted to do right then. "Please, Cade. *Please.*"

He swiftly snaked his right hand up between her breasts and gripped her opposite shoulder. "Hold on to the tailgate."

"Why?"

"To keep your hips from hitting the metal so hard I bruise you. I won't mark you that way," he said, voice rumbling against her back.

Sweet hell on fire. She gripped the tailgate and pulled her hips off.

She glanced over her shoulder as lightning flashed again, the strobe exposing his hot gaze locked on her backside. Then he pressed his broad head to her folds, and her legs buckled, shoving her onto his length and drawing a shout from both of them.

Cade grabbed her hips and, with care, worked his way

into her tight channel. He was so large it almost hurt, stretching her to the point she whimpered, then gasped.

He froze. "Okay?" When she didn't immediately answer, he began to retreat.

"Don't!" she cried. She shoved backward, taking him all the way to the hilt. Then she began to ride him, ignoring the almost-painful friction, sure her walls would adjust. They had to. But Lord save her, he was *huge*.

Cade took over, stroking her slower, pushing one leg up to give him better access and whispering things she only caught fractions of, things like, "Beautiful, stunning, tight, sexy, hell."

They were simple words of praise from a complicated man, and the offerings meant the world to her. But soon she gave up trying to hear him as he worked her body like a master painter worked a canvas, taking it from a blank slate to the very thing it had always been meant to be. She was obviously supposed to be wanton under his touch, and that's just what she became. Writhing madly, she urged him to move faster and cursed him in frustration.

He chuckled—*chuckled!*—and suggested she slow down.

"I don't *want* slow," she ground out even as she pushed at him.

His movements slowed even more. "Don't tell me what you want, Emmaline Graystone. I want your deepest desires, darkest cravings, the things you can't live without," he demanded in a voice that was accompanied by a commanding thrust of his hips.

She mewled, fighting to find her voice, to admit what she most craved. But her voice wouldn't come.

He drove into her harder, only to slow down as the

sensations she craved began to build, layering one atop another. "Answer me, Emma."

"I need to let go!"

He released every ounce of restraint he'd shown her. He tightened his grip and pushed into her, bringing her release rushing to the surface, the flood of pleasure rippling through her core in waves.

As lightning continued to flash and thunder rolled, wind whipped through the trees and made the rain sting everywhere it struck her bared skin.

He bent his knees and wedded her bare back to his chest, thrusting up into her. Then he slipped his fingers into her core and found her swollen clitoris. She came apart in his arms again.

Head thrown back, she opened her mouth and cried out into the deluge of rain.

He held her to him as he thrust once, twice, a third time, and then let loose what could only be called a roar of satisfaction.

She shook as he did, her legs giving out and leaving him to support her.

Cade scrambled to get ahold of her rain-slicked skin, finally shifting her around and settling her on the tailgate in a lumbering, far less graceful maneuver than he'd pulled earlier.

Settling between her legs, he rested his forehead against hers. His hot breath skated over her chilled skin. With infinite tenderness that surprised her, he ran his hands through her hair and simply held their heads together. Then he retrieved his hat and settled it on her head, smiling as she was forced to tilt the brim up in order to see him.

"You definitely earned the right to wear that," he murmured, zipping his pants.

"What right?"

"A cowboy never lets anyone wear his hat. *Anyone.* Unless it's a woman he wants to bed or has bedded. It's a…" He searched for the words, his brow creasing. "Not sure what it is, really. Not a tradition. Just a thing, I guess. It's a way to advertise to other men to keep their hands off his…the woman."

Emma's stomach sank a little. As far as she was concerned, this had been a onetime thing between them, a way to burn off the tension so they could work together. It wasn't some…*claiming.* She was no one's territory to mark. The fight to become her own woman in a profession dominated by men had been too long and too brutal to give in now. She claimed herself, and no man had the right to claim any part of her as his territory.

If he actually believed that his slapping his hat on her head marked her as off-limits, he had another think coming. But that could be cleared up later.

Right now? She had to come up with a plausible excuse for the condition in which she was going to arrive at the ranch. She had the distinct suspicion even the best explanation would be transparent.

Then there was the internal voice that grew louder and more certain with each passing day, her initial paranoia quickly becoming outweighed by clear evidence that said her business partner, Michael Anderson, was doing his level best to set her up to fail. If the information made its way back to him that she'd shown up at the Covington ranch looking like she'd been well loved in a tempestuous storm?

Michael would have the ammunition necessary to succeed.

5

AFTER THEY'D SET themselves to rights, they worked together to essentially drain the truck cab. Cade had been livid when he'd realized he'd forgotten to put the windows up. There was enough standing water for a goldfish to be quite happy.

Emma had silently rolled with it. Opening a suitcase in the backseat, she'd retrieved dry clothes and dressed without comment.

Cade hadn't had the option. He'd been forced to fold up the new saddle blanket he'd bought Reagan for her birthday and use it as a seat pad to keep his wet ass off the leather seats. Emma had also used the blanket to dry off and it now smelled of her.

They made their way to the highway at a much less frantic pace. He wasn't as anxious to get to the ranch now, sure there would be questions about their late arrival and the reason he, at least, was soaked through. He didn't want to ask Emma to lie about what they'd done, where they'd been or why they were late, but he also didn't want her subjected to his family's questioning. He'd end up getting pissed off and affirming what they would all most want to know about Emma—what was she to him?

He'd tell them she was the same to him as she was to them: a contractor and guest.

Liar, his mind whispered. *She's yours.*

Not funny, he responded with silent vehemence. *Not even* remotely *funny*. Cade didn't believe in love. It didn't transcend all things but, like everything else, had an expiration date. He had only to consider his mother's short life as proof.

Emma rode quietly, her gaze focused somewhere beyond the reach of the headlights as they sped down the highway. Full dark had fallen, the storm blowing off to the northeast as they drove almost due west. Without streetlights or the occasional flashes of lightning, the most he could make out were brief glimpses of pale skin when the rare oncoming car lit her up.

He was desperate to understand where she'd retreated to in that sharp mind of hers.

"You're tapping your nail to a silent beat. What song is running through your head?"

She twitched, and then seemed to force herself to glance his way, her pupils wide in the dim dash lights. "Pardon?"

"You object to a little pillow talk?"

"Pillow talk?" The question, a mere two words, was almost entirely devoid of emotion.

"You know. Talking after having se—"

"Right," she all but shouted. "Right." Softer this time. "Just trying to decide how I'm going to cover for my appearance when we get to the ranch. No doubt an explanation will be necessary."

He shrugged. "Far as I'm concerned, we had a flat tire and you got out to help me. Stepped into the bar ditch and fell, ruined your clothes and got soaked in the process. You changed and here we are."

"That easy?" she asked.

"Pretty much."

"I despise lying," she said on a heavy exhalation. "Unfortunately, I haven't come up with a way around it, given our situation."

Lying bothered Cade, too, but surprisingly not as much as Emma calling what they'd shared a "situation." They'd address that later. For now, if a small fib protected her from a country-style interrogation and good old-fashioned ribbing? He'd issue a thousand lies to spare her, small *or* large.

His shoulders tightened at her accusatory tone. "What's bugging you, Emma?"

She closed her eyes and huffed out a short laugh. "I'm trying desperately to focus on what's immediately in front of me, like composing ideas for the new travel trifold brochure for the ranch." She popped her knuckles one by one, swift and efficient. "I'm also considering highly exclusive events a few times a year for those willing to pay a premium for the experience."

She continued to talk about all the events and advertising material she had planned. She also wanted to write up press announcements to distribute to different media outlets before the end of her two weeks here. "That should generate an initial rush of interest, so the ranch will need to be prepared with software for managing reservations."

"We should save this conversation for the entire family's input," he said when she paused to catch her breath.

"I...well, I guess I wanted to explain what I was planning. I'd hoped you could give me some feedback on whether or not these kinds of things are in line with your family's ideals."

"You're asking for my input?" Surprise rang in his every word.

"Why wouldn't I?" She shifted, focusing her attention on him. "You understand your family's true vision for the ranch. You made it clear earlier you have a defined idea of what you want when it comes to the end result. Share your goals. Give me the best chance possible to be successful. Tell me what reservation software you're using, what your expectations are for repeat visits, referrals, corporate affairs and such. We need to develop a stronger game plan that covers these issues and more, and we're really under the gun to get it done before the inaugural event."

"You're proposing a hell of a lot of change all at once. We have two weeks, Emma—two *weeks*—before the first guests arrive. And as far as reservation software goes? We're using a calendar and pencil to track requests and keeping receipts in an envelope clipped to Eli's Day-Timer."

She slumped into her chair, eyes wide. "You can't run a big business that way."

"That's the point," he said gently. "This shouldn't be treated the same as a big business. This is an intimate venture, and we intend to keep it that way."

"But...paper and pencil? Even small businesses work better with appropriate technology. Something as easy as scheduling software and QuickBooks for accounting would make your lives so much easier. Those two things won't take away from the intimacy of the experience. Trust me."

"We can talk about it when we're all together."

"Fair enough." She hesitated. "Paper and pencil. I'm

feeling a little sick. Is there anything else I should be aware of? You know, before I get there and make a total ass of myself?"

"Just keep in mind that, besides Eli, the rest of us have always been pretty simple people. We're as fiercely loyal to each other as we are resistant to change."

"Great. So if I can find a way to ensure you don't have to use a computer, upgrade to satellite internet or serve anything but beef from your kitchens, your family might be receptive my ideas?"

"I'm going to pretend you didn't infuse that question with sarcasm." It was all he could do to keep the smile off his face.

Emma leaned her head against the headrest and closed her eyes. "Pretend away. I'm going to silently brainstorm ways to chisel guest receipts into stone. I have a good connection at UPS. Maybe I can get a deal on shipping the stone tablets to guests as keepsakes after they've gone home."

Cade chuffed out an involuntary laugh. He admired her grit. Seriously, how could he not?

"Laugh away, chump," she continued. "I'm going to have you computer literate and making online reservations before I leave," she groused.

"You'd be better off spending your days teaching a pig to fly as you would getting me to use a damned computer."

"We'll see," she said with far too much confidence for his comfort.

The quiet that fell between them then was comfortable, even easy. It gave Cade a chance to realize he'd been an ass. For all they'd shared, nothing excused his behavior. He'd been mostly responsible for what had gone down between them. He'd tried for suave, tried to come across as somewhat sophisticated, but he was sure even his best efforts were pathetic in the face of Emma's worldliness. It struck him then, what made them different. The woman had *class*—the kind of polish that couldn't be manufactured.

The idea they might have a little something together while she was here had been a delusion. What an utter fool he'd proven himself to be.

But he still wanted her. It clouded his mind, made his brain short-circuit. It was annoying, being so out of control over a woman he didn't really know—even after he'd been so incredibly intimate with her. And yeah, it had been intimate.

He wasn't the love 'em and leave 'em type. That was his little brother's MO. Cade was privately referred to as Father Covington by a group of single women in the area because he never got involved with anyone. And here he'd taken a near-perfect stranger over the tailgate of his truck in the middle of a rainstorm. Not just any stranger, either, but one he assumed was far more accustomed to silk sheets and five-star hotels, not the nature experience he'd given her. There was no way she'd be interested in him after that.

Doesn't stop you from wanting her all over again, his subconscious whispered.

"Shut up," he muttered.

Emma glanced at him. "Pardon?"

"Forget it. Talking to myself." *And doesn't* that *quite nicely sum up the head case you've become in the few hours since you met her?*

Cade focused on the road, watching with a growing sense of unease as the shadowy outline of the Bar C's main gate was revealed in the headlights' glow.

They were here.

EMMA WISHED MORE of the ranch was visible. She was curious about where Cade came from. After his very, *very* personal welcome, she was curious about who he really was when he wasn't seducing the pants—or little black dress—off some wide-eyed, holy-crap-he's-all-man city girl.

He'd gone from somewhat conversational to absolute silence the moment they passed under the ranch's sign. The farther down the wide dirt road they went, the thicker the tension in the cab became. She rolled down her window and reveled in the night. Besides the sound and light from the truck, silence ruled supreme out here. Then the forlorn mooing of a cow reached her, eliciting a wide smile.

"What?" The surly question drew her attention away from the window and to Cade's chiseled face, his expression made all the more harsh by the dash lights.

"Nothing. It's just…"

"Just what?" he asked in the same tone.

"No need to be a jerk. It's just that I've never heard a cow moo until now."

He reached up and settled his hat tighter to his head, small wisps of hair flipping out from under the band. "It's called lowing when they bawl like that."

"Good to know." Deflating a little, she peered out the window in time to see a brown body dart away from the truck. A cold chill ran up her spine. "What was that?"

Cade lifted one shoulder in an approximation of a shrug. "Coyote."

"As in Wile E.?" She hung out the window, trying to get a better look.

"As in 'kills newborn calves before their mamas can get up to defend them,'" he answered.

Well, *that* had squashed the goodwill she'd felt toward

her favorite childhood underdog. "Thanks for that happy image," she murmured, rolling up her window.

"I just don't want you getting the idea that life out here is all fun and games. It can be dangerous and there are things that might hurt you, things you'd never see coming."

"What, like you?" The calm of her voice surprised her. She'd imagined the words emerging as a shouted accusation. "Is this your way of warning me you're going to hurt me before this is all over?"

"No." He sighed heavily. "I didn't mean it that way."

They rounded a corner and Emma sucked in a breath. The clouds parted and the full moon shone down, lighting the world in monochromatic depths even Ansel Adams wouldn't have been able to adequately capture. Besides, it was a solely personal view, not something to be preserved or mass-produced. But, in this case, it could be shared.

That she sat next to Cade as the heavens revealed the scale of her surroundings meant something. She wasn't sure what. But the outlines of cedar trees, the evenly spaced fence posts and gleaming barbed wire, the black bodies of cows whose white faces made them seem headless in the eeriest of ways, to the moonlight sparking off the fast-moving creek—she shared it all with Cade.

He slowed to a stop, staring at her as she tried to take it all in, to assign the moment appropriate value. But she couldn't. The whole of it was too large. Forcing her gaze away, she shifted to meet Cade's stare. "It's so beautiful."

"So are you."

"Sweet talker." She opened the door and stepped out onto the dirt road. The night air was crisp, colder than she expected, and she shivered.

"People often don't realize it gets cold out here in

the desert at night," he said, moving around the rear of the truck and stepping in close behind her. "When the clouds disappear, it'll get even colder." Cade settled a hand at her waist.

She stepped out of reach, putting distance between them.

He let her go. "Living in the city, you create your own microclimate because of all the high rises and the cement, steel and glass. We don't have that out here, so we're more at Mother Nature's mercy."

She nodded, only half listening. It would be lovely to lean into him, to let him ease the tension building in her so she could regain her footing. But she couldn't rely on him. Not ever.

That didn't stop her from asking the one thing she most wanted to know. "What does this mean?"

He ignored the question, pointing so she shifted slightly to follow his gesture. A subtle glow hovered around the next rise. "Those are the lights from the main ranch house. It's where the barn, stables and bunkhouses are. That last building is where the cowboys live. The new guest bunks are situated near it so they have their own space but are part of the regular activity."

It irritated her that he'd ignore her question regarding where they stood, but she played along. For now. "How many cowboys do you have on staff?"

"They're more family than staff," he said, his voice soft. "There are a total of five cowboys on payroll. The number fluctuates around the seasons. For example, we bring in day workers in the fall when we gather and ship the cattle."

"Day workers?"

"Cowboys from both neighboring ranches and those who are on the move, looking for work. They're employed on a day-by-day basis for a flat fee. It's usually around seventy-five dollars per day, paid in cash." He shrugged and shoved his hands in his jeans pockets. "Not much considering they'll work sunup to sundown, but we'll feed 'em and see to their horses. Even provide a ride if they need one."

The idea of making seventy-five dollars for a day of hard labor stunned her. "How can anyone make a living on that?"

Cade stared out over the plains. "You have to want it bad enough to make the sacrifices that come with living the life."

She leaned a hip against the truck, wrapping her arms around herself. Was she wrong to say that seventy-five dollars wasn't much for a hard day's work? With all that had gone on lately, it seemed she should have learned to temper her words, particularly with the threat of Michael's ambition looming over her head.

Cade had withdrawn, his gaze focused on something in the distance.

"Something wrong?"

"There's no shame in a cowboy's life or the money he makes." Silence followed his words.

Yep, Emma had sailed across that invisible line between carelessness and tact, stepping right into immediate apology territory. She crossed her arms under her breasts and then tightened her hold. "I'm sorry if I crossed a personal boundary or asked you a question without first performing the secret handshake." She tipped her chin up and stared at the sky. "Help me figure out the differences between our lives, Cade. And, if you can, cut me a break in the process. This is my first ranch experience, and we're going to have to work together through the entire thing."

He moved nothing but his eyes when he finally looked at her. "Life out here isn't based on martini lunches and penthouse living. I don't expect you to truly understand, but I do expect you to temper your comments and respect our way of life."

Stunned, she stared at him, mouth working silently as she said a thousand silent things—defensive, definitely offensive, undoubtedly hurt. Who did he think she was? Short of the very little they'd shared, he knew nothing of her, nothing of where she came from.

Thankful the dark cloaked the riot of emotions playing out on her face, she dropped her chin and climbed into the truck, slamming the door. "If that's your perception of me as a businesswoman and, worse, a human being, I have absolutely no idea why you hired me. We might all be happier if you took me to the airport. Now."

6

CADE CROSSED HIS arms and leaned on the sill of the truck's open window. "Hear me out, Emma. I don't want anything but the truth between us."

"What's to stop you from lying? You don't owe me anything," she whispered.

"I want to be sure I don't hurt you in any way." He leaned in, ran a hand around her neck and pulled her to him, kissing her lightly. Her face was openly painted with surprise when he pulled away, but he didn't pause, didn't give her time to think. "I was initially opposed to hiring you because I wasn't convinced we could afford you. Money's tight after the outbreak we had last year that cost us so much in livestock and our own savings. We pay our bills, but there isn't much extra floating around after the last check is signed." What he said next was a personal revelation he hadn't intended to make but one she had to understand. "Also, I was, and maybe am, afraid that someone from New York wouldn't understand our heritage or our way of life. You'd come out here and do your advertising thing. We'd not only lose our privacy but end up being put on display like some kind of specimen of days long past. It's not the kind of attention I ever wanted to draw."

Her gaze softened. "I understand."

"But that's just it. I'm not sure you can. I hardly get it myself, so how could I expect you to understand them?" He strode away from the truck only to round on his heel and come back even faster than he'd left. "I can't lose who I am to this endeavor. My brothers don't think about it the same way because they have other identities. Eli's a lawyer. Tyson's an accomplished horseman and has an up-and-coming breeding program gaining regional recognition. Hell, even Eli's fiancé, Reagan, is a large-animal vet."

"And what about you? Where do you fit?" she asked tenderly.

"I'm just me, and this is my place. *This* is where I fit."

"Who are you, Cade?"

"I'm a simple cowboy, Emma. I'm the man who works for seventy-five dollars a day to make a little extra money now and again. The man who's up before dawn and typically isn't inside until dusk. The one who takes pride in a hard day's work and a job well done. The one who worries about keeping the ranch in the family, keeping that family's collective head above water."

"Sounds like quite a man, actually." Reaching through the open window, she gently rubbed his arm.

"I'm not entirely admirable," he grumbled, stepping out of her reach.

She managed to get hold of his wrist and stop his retreat. "No one I know is entirely admirable, Cade. People might act in what they believe is their—or someone else's—best interest, but rarely do they consider every possible aspect, every possible result. It just isn't possible, but it doesn't justify deeming my admiration of you unwarranted." Pausing, she searched his face. A flash of emotion passed through her eyes before she tipped her chin up and focused on him like he was the only person in the world. "Can I ask you something?"

"At this point, I'll give you my statistics without batting an eye. I wear a thirty-five by thirty-eight Wrangler MWZ jean, size thirteen boots and a men's tall shirt with an eighteen-inch neck. Oh, and I prefer boxer briefs."

She grinned. "I already got a demonstration of that last part."

"Suppose you did."

"No, what I wanted to ask is if, having met me, you believe I'm the best person for this job."

He hated himself for hesitating, but he wasn't sure how to answer that.

Squeezing his arms lightly, she nodded. "Let's get to the main house and talk to the rest of your family about whether or not I should be here, okay? If you believe someone else would better suit your end game, I'll gladly make some calls and find someone with more experience in this particular field."

Cade rounded the truck and hoisted himself into the driver's seat. Resting his hand on the key, he shook his head, closing his eyes. "I don't regret meeting you."

"Meeting me and hiring me are two different things." She started to reach for him and stopped herself, instead settling her hands in her lap. "The point here is that the best marketing and public relations person never allows a client's true self to become lost in a campaign. We create plans that, in a very real way, exploit who you all are as both a group and as individuals. We sell your surroundings, your core beliefs, the things that make you different from your competitors. This may drive business to your doorstep, but I'm not sure you or your brothers realized what they were in for in hiring a firm like mine. Or, in the end, whether it was something they want."

"Emma—" he started, but she interrupted him.

"In that case, the ranch never should have hired my firm and Michael never should have accepted the retainer or subsequent payments. But we'll talk about all that at the house." She leaned her head against the doorframe and took in the vast landscape. But the truck's engine remained off, ticking as it cooled. "Seriously, Cade. Let's go. I'm at the point I have to determine whether I should be sending initial impressions to the staff assigned to this project or call the airline to change my return flight to tomorrow."

From the corner of her eye, she watched him study her. She sat there and let him, too tired to fight with him about finishing the trip, getting this over with. Because when the brothers realized it would be *their* images, *their* lives plastered over the pages of both print and digital media versus that of models and Photoshopped backgrounds, that they'd be approached with all kinds of offers if they all looked as delicious as Cade? Chances were beyond favorable that she'd find herself in New York by noon tomorrow.

His voice split the darkness with a ferocity she hadn't expected. "You're the one who came out here and said you'd do the two weeks to make sure we're ready for guests. You leave now—we've got no one to make sure this goes off without a hitch."

Twisting around on the leather seat, she was shocked to find him out—scowling her. "Pardon?"

"If I have to, I'll call you on your word. 'Love or loathing' ring a bell?"

Stomach knotted, she gave a single nod. He'd mentioned he was worried about the money. She refused to consider what he might do to save some cash, how far he'd take it to win their silly bet. "The bet is off. If your brothers decide hiring my firm was a mistake, I'll refund the money you've already paid."

His eyes flared, and then faded to a flat blue. "That'd be right kind of you."

"Isn't that what you're after? Some reassurance I'm not going to run off with your money? We have a contract, Cade. I'm sure that Eli, being a lawyer and highly skilled negotiator, went over the terms thoroughly and built in an exit clause for either or both of us." She tried to smooth her spiky hair into some semblance of a professional presentation. Taking a moment to collect her thoughts, she shifted her body so their shoulders were square. "But until we're sure exactly how the rest of your family feels about me executing my obligations, we have nowhere to go but forward."

With that, she settled into her seat and waited for him to start the truck so they could get this over with.

CADE PARKED IN front of the main house. The porch light was on, the sounds of construction absent due to the late hour. Rounding the front of the truck, he opened Emma's door and helped her down before retrieving her luggage from the crew cab's backseat.

"Thought you'd forgotten your way home when you didn't…" Eli called as he opened the front door, his wide-eyed gaze skipping from Cade to Emma. By the time his eyes rested on Cade again, his face was cool, emotionally detached, even. "Ms. Graystone, I'd like to invite you inside. Reagan!" he shouted, never looking away from Cade. "You, I'll talk to in the barn."

Yep. Conversation would be held in the language of fists with subtitles provided in English.

Emma stepped forward, holding a hand out to Eli. "Mr. Covington, it's nice to meet you."

Furious, but stumped by years of professional protocol, Eli shook her hand. "And you as well, Ms. Graystone."

"Please, call me Emma." She gestured between herself and Cade. "I realize we're a mess and it would be very easy to make improper assumptions, but allow me to reassure you that it's not what it seems."

She met Eli's silent, questioning stare with cool confidence.

Emma pressed on. "Cade stopped at my request to help an elderly couple with Ohio plates during the middle of a thunderstorm. He got out in the torrential rain and, not wanting to be the diva who'd ask him to stop yet not offer to help herself, I followed." She shook her head and smiled in a self-deprecating manner. "Being from Manhattan, I would have been highly efficient in hailing them a cab. I'm sure you're stunned to learn there were no cabs available tonight."

"This true?" Eli directed the question to Cade.

"If you're questioning the woman's account, you should ask her, not me."

Emma stepped forward again, the movement somehow more authoritative that the initial steps she'd taken. "There are many things I'll tolerate, Mr. Covington. Asking your brother if I'm lying while I'm standing right here? That *isn't* one of them. If you have an issue with the information I'm relaying, I'd ask—and expect—that you have the courtesy to address me directly."

Cade nearly swallowed his tongue. She hadn't denied lying to Eli but had efficiently and politely demanded his respect.

"I like her already." Eli's fiancée stepped around him

and offered Emma her hand. "I'm Reagan and, for better or worse, I'm engaged to the jackass impinging your honor."

Blushing, Emma stepped forward and around Eli to shake the other woman's hand. "I'm Emmaline Graystone, but I'd love it if you'd call me Emma."

"Pleased to meet you, Emma. Did you two stop for supper on your way here?"

"No. There wasn't really an opportunity. My idea of remote is a four-block hike to Chinese takeout. Here, apparently, 'remote' is more than one hundred miles without the opportunity for even a vending machine. I have some suggestions regarding that—simple ideas such as packing a snack or meal for your guests, particularly those with children. Say, cheese, crackers and a summer sausage along with bottled water for your adults, and something like apples, smaller crackers and string cheese with a juice box for each child."

She fisted her hand over her stomach, and Cade's guilt surged. He hadn't fed her. Before he could comment, though, she smiled wide. "New York truly never sleeps, so you can get food twenty-four-seven. But at this point? I'd settle for that string cheese and juice box. I'd even beg."

"You're entitled to far more than a juice box after the evening you've had. Come on in and I'll reheat dinner for you." Reagan pulled Emma up the steps, calling to Cade, "You, too, cowboy. You never miss a meal, so I'd imagine you're near to wasting away. To the kitchen, troops."

"Reagan?" Cade said gently.

The woman paused in her efficient rounding up of humans—and her circumvention of Eli's interrogation—to look at him.

"I would imagine, worn out as we both are, a shower before dinner would be welcomed."

She grinned and winked at him while Eli's back was turned. "You're right. Emma, I'll see you to your room and let you get showered and changed. I'll have dinner waiting when you're finished."

Cade wasn't entirely surprised to see Emma falter on the steps, so close to tripping Reagan was compelled to grab her arm and steady her. She glanced at Cade.

"We would have put you in a guest cabin," he explained, aiming for a neutral tone, "but right now we're waiting on the county to come out and clear the electrical and the plumbing so we can get our certificates of occupancy."

Her lips thinned. "You don't have your certificates of occupancy," she said slowly. "On how many units?"

Cade bristled. "Well, if I don't have anywhere to put you, it only makes sense that—"

"I don't want to pick apart details as you avoid the question. Simply tell me exactly how far from ready you are for guests. I believe that will justify the temper I'm about to unleash."

He stepped in close and bent down, going nose to nose with her. "What, exactly, do you assume we've been doing out here *besides* busting our asses to be ready for the opening date *your firm* suggested?"

"A date one of your people signed off on. Give me a second and I can tell you who it was," she retorted. "I've got your entire file scanned and available."

"I signed it," Eli muttered.

The slight wisp of a woman rounded on the significantly larger man. "Doesn't matter whose name is on the line. You agreed for the ranch as a whole, Mr. Covington. Beginning tomorrow, I'll sit down with your team to go through your contractor, vendor and supplier lists and your punch list for each." Eli took a deep breath, but she held up what Cade believed would quickly come to be known as The Hand of Shush. "Both explanations and excuses are irrelevant at—" she glanced at her watch "—nearly ten o'clock at night. If I can make a sandwich to take to my room, grab a quick shower and crawl into bed, we can start tomorrow at 7:00 a.m."

Cade moved forward. "We usually have breakfast about an hour earlier."

She met his gaze, all intimacy between them hidden deep enough he questioned whether or not he'd imagined the whole thing. When she finally spoke, her words were corporate-crisp. "Tomorrow? Breakfast is at seven."

Taking her suitcases from him, she said to Reagan, "If you'll show me to my temporary room, I'll dump my bags and grab that shower. The sandwich may just have to wait since I wouldn't want this kind of filth in my own kitchen."

Reagan grinned. "Now I don't *think* I'm going to like you. I *know* I am." Laughing, she took one of Emma's bags and started into the house before Cade could protest. "I'll put you in Eli's old room downstairs. There's a bathroom attached so you can grab that shower. I'll make you a sandwich and leave it just inside the door on the dresser while you're showering. That cool?"

"I might be a little in love with you."

"Nah. You just love me for my efficiency."

The women laughed, and Cade's brows winged down as he watched them disappear down the hall and around the corner to the stairs, chattering all the way. "Why do I feel like I just got my ass handed to me but Reagan got a gold star?"

Eli shoved his hands in his pockets, shoulders hunched.

"Probably because our asses were just parked on the chopping block. But Reagan played the Female Solidarity card. We can't hang with that."

"I guess not." Cade shook his head. "Why'd Reagan have to put her downstairs?"

Eli rounded on him slowly. "About that…"

"I'm tired and I'm hungry. Just leave the whole thing alone."

"I'm going to want details."

"Said every man who suspects sex is involved in a story." Cade ran his hands through his hair.

"Is it?"

"Wouldn't you like to know," Cade murmured, moving past Eli and into the house.

What Reagan had told Emma was true. There *was* a bathroom attached to Eli's old room—a Jack-and-Jill type bath that was linked to another room.

His.

7

EMMA STRIPPED DOWN to the skin and stepped into the bathroom, locking both doors before starting the shower. Adjusting the water temperature to somewhere near "sanitize," she slipped under the spray and cursed the heat until she acclimated. Then she grabbed the bar of soap and washrag Reagan had provided. Scrubbing seemed insufficient. Sandblasting would be so much more appropriate given the travel grime that clung to her.

Not even her current level of grunge could stop her from appreciating the way her muscles had been truly well used. There was only one person, one *man*, to thank for that.

Cade.

She parked her palms on the front shower wall and let the water pound into her shoulders. *What am I going to do about him?*

They'd shared something incredible tonight, something the likes of which she'd only read about when she indulged in a hot romance novel. This, though? This had been the real deal.

A shiver that had nothing to do with water temperature and everything to do with sensory memory rolled through her. It started at her head and raced to her feet, curling her toes. The man's skills should come with a serious warning.

Her hand traced the contour of one breast. Her nipple pearled as she imagined it was Cade's hand touching her, Cade's hand caressing her.

What was stopping her from having more than that one incredible encounter? She could have a short, illicit fling. Women in her office were always engaged in such things. The few friends she had seemed to have either been with one man forever or were forever changing men. Why couldn't she be one of them? Why couldn't *she* be the one they envied as they sat around a Sunday morning brunch table relaying the week's hardships— and exploits? Her breathing grew heavier. If Cade were willing, *she could be that woman.*

A harder shiver raced through her at the mental image, followed by a sharp knock on the bathroom door. Expecting Reagan with the shampoo and conditioner she'd asked to borrow—something she'd forgotten to pack on her hasty exit from New York—Emma stuck her head around the curtain and called out, "Come in."

Cade stepped through the door. Shirtless. The man was shirtless.

It was the first time she'd had the opportunity to consider him in full light. If Edison hadn't been dead, she'd have sent a thank-you card, because damn, the man was a thing of hard lines and rough beauty. Her fingers curled into her palms with the urge to touch him, to trace the sinewy length of arms, the peaks and valleys of that muscular chest and the ripped abs. She wanted to taste the salt on his skin with less frenzy, savoring every nip and bite and soothing caress.

"Brought down the sandwich. It's on the dresser in

your room. Also, Reagan said you need shampoo and conditioner. There's a brand-new bottle down here. It's one of those two-in-one things." He dug around under the sink. "Here it is." He stood and made to offer her the bottle, freezing mid-gesture. "Emma?"

She could only imagine what he saw when he considered her—makeup gone, hair wet, her skin pale. Shaking her head, she held out the hand not clutching the shower curtain to her chest. "Thanks for the sandwich and shampoo." Her words were so soft they were nearly lost in the patter of water from the showerhead and the constant hum of the bathroom fan.

Cade didn't move.

She smiled a little at his fumble.

"Anything else I can get you?"

His words were drenched in sensual promise and she shivered again. What she wanted to do with him in a shower—*this* shower—would no doubt make him blush to the roots of his hair. "I'm pretty sure what I'd ask for isn't on the menu, especially with your family sleeping upstairs."

His blue eyes darkened and his hand went to his belt buckle and paused. "My parents had heavy insulation put between the floors. There's no threat we'll be disturbed."

She nibbled her bottom lip, thrilling when his gaze landed there and his pupils expanded. Well, she'd wanted a fling. "Lose the pants, cowboy."

He shucked his jeans and slipped into the shower, his hungry stare roaming over her body with unchecked desire. "Turn around, hands flat on the wall."

She complied, the hot water pounding against her as she planted her hands on the tile.

Cade pressed his hard body against hers. He molded the line of his chest to her back and settled the thick, hard length of his cock against her, sliding slightly. Water flowed over their bodies and found its way into the crevices between his ridges of muscle and the column of her spine. Their skin grew slippery.

What was it about this man and water?

In a swift movement, he slipped his hands under hers where they remained on the tile wall. It was the work of a moment to twine their fingers together, curling his hands into fists. Then he stood up, pulling her with him as he crossed his arms over her chest and held her that much closer to him.

Emma spun and dropped to her knees. She stroked his cock, root to tip. Resting a hand on his hip to help keep her balance, she slowly fed the length of him down her throat, as deep she could take him. She risked a glance up.

Eyes wild, he'd pushed his damp hair off his forehead and held it in fistfuls as he watched her with absolute awe. "I thought… I mean, I didn't think… I'm pretty sure I don't…why are you…best ever…want you so bad…sweet hell…don't want to ruin…" His eyes fluttered closed, but the scrambled fragments from his mouth didn't. And the harder she worked him, the faster he babbled.

Finally, she pulled back with a single lick to the very tip of his shaft. "I don't remember you being such a talker, Mustang Sally."

"Mustang Sally?" he asked, face slack as his gaze went from his cock in her hand to her mouth and back.

"You called me Manhattan. Mustang Sally was the first thing that came to mind at the moment." She grinned. "We'll just shorten that to Sally to keep it easy for everyone."

"You can do—" he flapped a hand, eyes wild—"*that* and still *think*?"

"Advantage of being a woman. Giving amazing head doesn't switch off my common sense *or* my brain. Also gives me the chance to figure out my next move."

Cade reached for her, but she moved faster than he did. Emma closed her lips over the swollen head of his erection and again swallowed down as much of his length as she could, working her way down and then up to the tip. Cupping and massaging his testicles very gently with one hand, she maintained her balance with the other.

He gripped her head, encouraging her efforts with unabashed enthusiasm. His hips pumped, thrilling her that she could drive him to this level of pleasure so quickly.

Slipping a couple of fingers into her own heat, she began stroking the tight knot of nerves there. She whimpered around his thickness.

Wide eyed, Cade watched her and, realizing what she doing, groaned. He tried to pull away. "I can't, Emma. I can't hold on…can't hold out. You have to stop."

She shook her head, working him over with her mouth even as she deftly manipulated herself. The crest of orgasm built, driving her toward the pinnacle.

Strong hands gripped her under her arms and pressed her against the wall. "Legs around my waist. Fast."

She managed to get her legs around him even though his skin was slippery.

"I'm clean. No sex since I was last tested. You still want me to get a condom?" he asked, voice tighter than piano wire. "Because I will."

"Same. Haven't had a lover. Three years. Tested twice since. Celibate. On birth control. Can't wait." She spoke in broken sentences and didn't, couldn't, care. "Now,

Cade. Now." Reaching between them, she guided him to her core.

He slid in with one solid shove.

She bit the soft spot between his shoulder and neck to muffle her shout. He was large, she was sore and the two succeeded in making her positively quake in his arms.

Cade hesitated. "Emma?"

"Move," she pleaded.

Spreading his feet and bending his knees, he dug his fingers into her skin. He retreated only to pull her down so his shaft scraped her clitoris. Over and over he withdrew only to drive into her with tenuous restraint.

He could have given her no more than half a dozen strokes or as many as a hundred. Emma had no idea. All she knew was that between heartbeats, her orgasm crashed through her, wave after wave. Heat poured through her as every muscle she owned seized, tightened and refused to let go. She threw her head back, banging it against the shower wall, but she didn't care. Nothing could override the pleasure washing through every cell in her body. Nothing could stop the second orgasm that followed fast on the heels of the first.

Never. Never had this happened to her.

Cade stiffened with a groan, the tendons in his neck standing out in stark relief. The movements of his hips were no longer sure and powerful but instead unpredictable and jerky.

She watched his face as he came. It struck her that she'd never seen anything so raw, so powerful, so uninhibited in another human being as what this man was sharing with her right now.

When his hips finally stilled, he pulled away and settled her under the steaming water. He retrieved her washrag and resumed bathing her.

"You don't have to do that, Cade."

"Just one more chance to touch you," he answered, his breath hotter against the shell of her ear than even the steam. "And I'm not finished touching you."

"Regrettably, you are for the night."

His hand stilled over her belly button. "Pardon?"

"I still want to go over our PR plans tonight. Tomorrow's going to be a hell of a day without us staying up all night shaking the sheets."

He chuckled. "Heard it called a lot of things, but never that."

"Pays to be creative in my business." She finished rinsing off and got out of the shower, leaving him to finish up. When he emerged, she handed him a towel and met his bright eyes with what she was sure was a somber stare. "We have to talk about how this is going to happen with me working for you. I want you to understand I don't sleep with clients."

"Want me to fire you?" he asked with nonchalance as he toweled his hair dry.

"Not so much," she responded, a cold void dropping into her middle. *Would it be that easy for him?* "What I meant is that we have to establish some basic boundaries."

He looked up, grinning, until he seemed to realize she was serious. "What do you mean, 'boundaries'?"

"Your contractors and vendors won't deal with me if they even *suspect* I'm sleeping with you. You have to give me space to work during the day. Treat me like the hired help I am." At his blank face, the first pangs of fear resonated through her. "You said yourself that my company's finances have been rocky. If word gets around that I'm messing around with a client, it could ruin me."

"Messing around with any client or messing around

with someone like me?" His voice was flat, devoid of any and all emotion.

"Yes. No." She clutched her towel tighter. "Yes in that you're a client."

"And no?"

"In that…" She raked her fingers through her wet hair. "It's that you and I are so different, from different backgrounds, different values systems, different long-term goals and expectations. That I'm city to your country, I suppose." The steam-filled bathroom muffled the words, but not enough.

Cade propped a hip against the counter and crossed his arms over his chest. "Of all the things I considered you might say, that hadn't even really made the list. I suppose it should have." He folded his towel and hung it on the towel bar on what was apparently his side of the bathroom. Naked as the day he was born, he stepped through the doorway into his room. He paused and gave her his profile. "I figured you for a lot of things, but never someone who'd be scared to own her actions."

"I'm not scared to own whatever it is between us."

"Could've fooled me. Wait. You just did." He chuckled humorlessly. "Good night, Ms. Graystone."

"Don't do this, Cade," she said, starting toward his door.

"I'm not doing anything, darlin'. This is just me expressing to you that I have no intention of abiding by your 'boundaries.'" He shut the door to his bedroom and turned the lock.

CADE SLIPPED OUT of the house at about five-thirty the next morning. He hadn't slept a wink and was so tired he could hardly function. Didn't matter. He wasn't going to be anywhere near the group when the 7:00 a.m. meeting hit. Where she was concerned, he couldn't take much more. Every man had a breaking point, and he was ashamed he'd nearly reached his last night.

They'd all look on Emma with absolute delight. Eli would beam because it was his connection that had scored her taking on the event, no matter that the true reason she'd taken it was in an effort to generate more immediate revenue. She'd said so yesterday. Whatever was going on behind closed doors where her business was concerned hadn't hit the news. But they were clearly bleeding out on paper. Her credit rating had suffered, which meant her reputation wasn't far behind.

But her business wasn't the issue for him. She'd made him feel like a country hick, as if his values were too simple and his vision of home and hearth too pedantic compared to her high-rise, five-star-dining lifestyle.

That part wasn't what chapped his ass so badly, though. It was that she seemed ashamed of him for who he was. She knew where he'd come from. What's more, his family had opened their home to her at the last minute to ensure she had a clean, safe place to stay. And she'd called him "country to her city."

"Right," he huffed, digging his heels into the dirt and pulling against the broken fence post. "Might as well have called it 'crass versus class.'"

If that's what she thought, he might as well act the part. He intended to ride fence for the next week—he'd left a note for Eli explaining his brother shouldn't request Cade's return except for an emergency. He'd loaded provisions on one of the packhorses, mounted his own horse and taken off as the sun broke the horizon. Still, he hadn't been able to stop himself from one last glance over his shoulder as he crested the nearest hill. Emma's bedroom light was on.

He managed to convince himself not to go home and hash this out with her but continue on. She'd been clear last night; he was okay to fool around with, but damn him if he touched her in the light of day.

He should be better than that to her. And hell, he wanted her to see he *could* be better than that—that he was worth more than a nighttime fling. He wanted her to accept that he was worth the emotional investment.

Gently laying his spurs to his horse's side, he clucked at the pack animal and started down the far side of the hill. The two animals broke into an easy lope. Every stride carried him farther and farther away from the torment he'd left behind.

But he didn't experience the deep sense of relief he'd expected to find once he was free of her. He actually felt worse. Why, he had no idea, but he wasn't examining it too closely, either. This whole self-revelation thing had been great for Eli, but Cade had vowed he wouldn't fall victim to the same feminine expectation—that he change who he was in order to be the man she expected him to be. He'd never change.

He dropped the pack animal's lead and shoved his hat on his head. His horse grabbed the bit. Cade didn't fight him for it. They'd end up where they ended up, and they'd find their way back. Eventually. Right now? He needed to let off a little steam, and his good ole horse, Ziggy, seemed to understand.

They ran until both were lathered in sweat. Only then did Cade regain control of the situation, working the bit free and slowing the horse down to first a trot and then a walk. They'd covered an easy four miles and left the packhorse far behind. Chances were good the packhorse had headed for the barn. He'd show up there and people would worry something horrid had happened to Cade and then they'd call the—

The SAT phone rang as if on cue. With a deep sigh, he answered. "Yeah?"

"You're due at the kitchen table in about three minutes," his youngest brother, Ty, said. "We're all here, including the hottie."

"Want to keep your hands?"

"Uh…is this a trick question?"

"Keep your hands to yourself where the woman is concerned," Cade bit out, "and your hands are yours to do whatever you want with. Touch her and I'll cut 'em off."

"Bro, tell me you did *not* do the forbidden polka with Ms. McNaughty!"

"Shut up," Cade hissed. "It's none of your… 'The forbidden polka'?"

"Oh that's child's play. I've got some good ones, like Downward Dogging, knowing someone in the Biblical sense, working the mortar and pestle, crashing the—"

"Stop!" Cade couldn't help but grin and shake his head. "Where the hell do you get this stuff?"

"I get bored." Voices sounded in the background, and Cade heard Ty's boots on the floor as the younger man walked away. "You want me to tell them you'll be here?"

"No. There's fence down on pasture twelve and I've brought the stuff out to mend it. *Then* I'll be there." *She could stuff that in her pipe and smoke it.* "Ranch work has to come first."

"Yeah, well, this sort of *is* ranch work, Cade." Ty blew out a short, hard breath. "I get that it's tough to face a woman after you've done the whole paddling up Coochie Creek, but you've got to face the music."

"Not when the music amounts to a familiar banjo solo,

my brother," Cade murmured. "And if you offer one more euphemism for sex, I swear to all that's holy I will have you cleaning stalls for the next week."

"You're not my boss," his little brother snorted. "I'm one-third owner of this place."

"Trust me—you'll be cleaning those stalls."

Silence met his threat, then in a long-suffering tone he said, "Fine. I'll cover you. But get here as fast as you can. I don't want her having the contractors paint the shutters turquoise because it's 'trendy.'"

Cade couldn't help but laugh. "She's not the type, but I'll be there as soon as the fence is fixed."

"Why didn't you send someone else to do it?"

Cade sat quietly, focusing on further slowing his breathing.

"And why does Ziggy sound as if he's breathing hard enough to be used as industrial bellows?" Skepticism finally laced the kid's words. He might love his brothers, but to Ty? The horses were sacred.

"We had a good run, burned off some excess energy."

"You might be better off if you admitted the truth."

The quiet words put Cade's back up. "And just what would that be?"

"I suppose it's different for everyone."

"Yeah?" Cade snarled.

Ty huffed out a hard breath. "Let me know when you come to a conclusion. I could use the insight. Just…"

"Just what?"

"Open your eyes before you go throwing opinions or punches. Makes for a much better, far fairer fight if you know what you're really fighting about…or for." The phone clicked to signal the end of the call. Then the SAT phone beeped three times fast before the screen went blank.

Cade looked around at the place where he and his horse had finally come to a stop. One of the prettier places on the ranch, and he hadn't even noticed. His eyes had been open, but he hadn't seen. Was that what Ty had meant?

"I see a bunch of land and not enough cattle to make a living. The need to bring strangers in to fund our way of life. A PR and marketing firm we hired with borrowed money, a firm whose services may, or may *not*, pay enough in dividends to repay the loan. That's what I see."

He could recognize the problems fine. The real issue with the ranch and with Emma was that he had no way to control the outcome.

8

EMMA STARED OUT the front window of the main house as she contemplated the multitude of options at her disposal when it came to killing Cade. First, she really had to talk to him about some contractor issues and definitely resolve the delay in the furniture delivery. But after that? All bets were off.

It had been made clear at the morning meeting that Cade considered frugality a religion, and the expenses incurred for her firm's services went against his belief system. She'd already discerned as much from her conversations with him.

She was no stranger to living lean. When receivables had begun their decline over the past eighteen months, Emma had been forced to learn to live frugally in order to keep from losing her two-bedroom apartment on Seventy-second Street. By cutting back hard in her personal life and eating a lot of packaged noodle dinners, she'd been able to keep all her staff on. No one had lost his or her job because of the company's struggles. Now more than ever, she appreciated the true value of a dollar earned and a dollar saved.

But she also appreciated the effort she put into earn-

ing and saving that money. If Cade couldn't show her
that he respected the value of her work, she was going
to have a real issue with finishing this job.

And this contract had to go off without a hitch. The
guest list for the cattle drive event was full of names that
would help rebuild the firm's client roster into the robust
thing it used to be. By having these people witness her in
action, see the results of her efforts, she should be able
to generate a win-win for both the ranch and her company. All she had to do was ensure that every guest left
here with the surety that she was qualified to run an efficient PR and marketing campaign. Then she could figure out what the hell was going on with Michael. Prove
once and for all whether he was undermining her and,
if necessary, fire his ass.

However, if Cade was belligerent and made people
think he didn't want them there, if he was anything other
than welcoming, she was going to have a real fight on
her hands. So she had to make sure he was on board for
the grand opening, or she was going to pay someone to
truss him up and gag him while the ranch's first guests
were here. She couldn't allow him to destroy her efforts
with well-timed barbs or, worse, comments on her inef-
ficiency or some such nonsense.

She cringed. Her plans and expectations sounded both
militaristic and impersonal now, more so than they had
at the table this morning. Eli had been all about operating as she proposed, but he was a lawyer by education
and experience. The win-at-all-costs, general lack of
concern for other people's overall well-being, including Cade's individuality, was Michael's style. Not hers.
And that left her with the distinct sensation she needed
to shower. In bleach. It was almost over, though. This
event was going to get things on track. Then she could

operate the way Reagan and Ty did, with a more humanistic approach. She just couldn't afford to soften her resolve. Not for thirteen more days.

Which brought her full circle, because it meant getting Cade on board.

She lifted her coffee cup to her mouth, pausing halfway as a horse and rider topped the hill.

The horse was magnificent, broad and heavily muscled with a smooth gait and a sense of confidence she'd never known an animal could exude. His brown coat gleamed with sweat. His black mane and tail simply shone. When the cowboy called out to someone, the horse never faltered, just kept his forward momentum toward the barn. At an invisible directive from the cowboy, he slowed to a walk.

The man rode as if he'd been born in the saddle, relaxed and yet obviously in control. He was masculine grace personified—broad shoulders, narrow waist, chestnut-brown hair that shone in the sun when he removed his Stetson.

Cade.

Half of her wanted to stand there and watch him, unobserved, as he interacted with others, to discover the differences in how he treated her versus the others on the ranch. Did he show her any favor? Did it even matter? The last question was the deciding factor. Setting her coffee cup on the kitchen counter, she crossed to the foyer, slipped her feet in her designer cowboy boots and walked out the front door. He'd dismounted and disappeared into the barn, so she headed there. She hadn't made it thirty yards before a discreet wolf whistle sounded.

Someone hollered for the men to, "hold your comments to none, thanks." Glancing around, she spied Ty on the roof of one of the cabins, attaching the tin to the wood decking. Stomping over, she glared up at him.

"Don't glare at *me*," he said on a laugh. Then he pulled off his hat and slapped it against his leg before retrieving a bandana and wiping his brow. "Your problem client just went into the barn."

Emma had to admit Ty was attractive, and he ran this particular crew with efficiency and good humor. But it wasn't him who crowded her mind and kept her tossing and turning all night.

"What's with the wolf whistling?" she asked.

He shook his head and climbed down the ladder. "Ignore 'em. The best-lookin' thing they usually set their eyes on is me. Pretty woman shows up, they get a little out of control."

She couldn't help but laugh.

"That Cade's hat?" he asked quietly.

"I suppose it is, yes." She pulled it off, tracing a finger along the brim.

"Do me a favor, would you? He needs it because he'll be working out here most of today. I've got an extra hat in my truck. Wear mine until we can get you something of your own."

"Will I need a cowboy hat?"

"Chances are good."

She grinned. "You sound like a Magic 8 Ball."

"Wouldn't be the first time my balls have been called magic," he countered, returning the smile.

"Lord save us from Covington humility." Taking in all the trucks parked around, she hesitated. "I have no idea which one is yours."

He walked her to a very nice, newer model Ford four-wheel drive pickup, opened the door and crawled inside. The gun rack on the rear window didn't hold a rifle but instead a pristine black Stetson on one hook and a rope on the other. The hat he handed over. The rope he took down and kept.

"What's with the rope?"

He shrugged. "Insurance."

"You're the strangest man," she said, shaking her head.

"We'll see." He jerked his chin to the barn. "Now, go give him his hat and kick his ass. After his smart-ass remarks to me this morning, he deserves it."

"So I'm your muscle, huh?" she teased.

He flexed and she laughed. "Put those things away before someone gets hurt," she said lightly.

"I wouldn't hurt a fly, sweetheart."

"Hurt *feelings*. Not many men as pretty as you, cowboy." She reached up and chucked him under the chin, earning her a wide grin.

"You may have strange tastes in men, but at least you're not blind."

Laughing again, she spun on her heel and started toward the barn, switching hats as she walked.

CADE HOSED ZIGGY off behind the barn. When the horse was sufficiently cooled down, Cade took the flat side of a shedding blade and pulled as much water off Ziggy's coat as possible before taking him into his stall. There, Cade brushed him down with a soft brush, oiled his hooves and dumped some grain in the horse's feed trough. He included an amino acid supplement to help the horse recover faster from the morning's hard ride, guilt eating at him over having let the big guy run as he had without a truly proper warm-up. As a precaution, he decided to wrap his cannons. Then he'd...

Cade shook his head, ashamed of himself. He was hiding in the barn like some kid who knew he was going to get it for taking off when there were chores to do.

"To hell with that," he muttered. "I'm a grown man. I'll do as I see fit and take care of the ranch the way it's always been done."

"Right," said a familiar feminine voice, the drawl laced with a bite.

Cade spun so fast Ziggy shied away.

"Because to do it any other way could be dangerous," Emma continued. "It could result in sex in a thunderstorm, racing across pastures to hide in a copse of aspens, joining someone in a shower or even—"

"Enough," he bit out.

Hurt flashed in her eyes, and he wondered at it. For her to be hurt, it implied she'd given him some level of importance. And after what she'd said last night, that left him thoroughly confused.

She'd made it clear she considered them oil and water. She considered him water—basic, predictable, accessible, flip on a tap or flush a toilet and there he was, *common*. She was oil—superior, worldly, offered in specialty shops, flavorful. What had happened between them had been nothing more than a shake-up. Then they'd quickly returned to where she considered they belonged.

"Cade!"

His chin snapped up. "What?"

Emma's eyes narrowed. "Have you heard a word I said?"

"Had other things on my mind." Talking Ziggy down, he unbuckled the horse's halter and stepped out of the stall, closing it behind him. "Don't suppose you've got a CliffsNotes version of the lecture, do you? I've got things to do."

"I wasn't going to… That's a lie. I was going to lay into you for blowing off this morning's meeting."

"Had other things to do."

"Yesterday you talked about wanting to protect this way of life and not allow it to become some five-dollar pony show. If you're serious about that, or if you want the right to chew me out over how I handle this project, you have to show up to the meetings. Otherwise, as far as I'm concerned, you're giving me and your family carte blanche to do what we determine is best. In that case? You'll keep your complaints to yourself. Clear enough for you?"

He stepped into the tack room and hung the halter on the appropriate peg before stepping into the doorway and leaning against the door casing. "Why would I bother complaining? It's not as if you'll be here that long. I can hold my tongue till you're gone, then make the changes that I think need making."

Her eyes went wide. She opened her mouth but nothing came out. Instead of trying again, she flung the hat in her hands at him, Frisbee-style. "Go to hell, Covington." Spinning on her heel, she stalked away, her T-shirt tucked into Wrangler jeans so snug they left him wondering if he'd find a panty line if he ran his fingers over her rear.

Then reality struck. She'd thrown *his hat.* He snatched it up and started after her. "Emma, hold on."

She didn't stop, slow down or acknowledge him in any way.

"Why are you so upset?"

"Because I deserve respect—from *all* of you." She met his gaze head-on. "And instead? Eli questioning me when we first arrived, Ty making excuses for the contractors' wolf whistling and you…" She trailed off and looked away. "Enough said."

"Why did you? Lie, that is," he clarified when she shot him a quick, confused look. "Last night, you lied to Eli."

Gesturing to the hat with her chin, she said, "Might pick that up before the dirt makes it unsalvageable."

Spinning on her heel, she left him standing in the barn, hat in his hands.

9

EMMA'S SMALL BEDROOM window was open halfway to let the late-afternoon breeze into the cool basement room. So when the dinner bell sounded, sharp and *loud*, she came out of her skin.

"Gah!" she shouted, scattering papers and nearly tossing her laptop.

"Dinner's ready," said a familiar male voice through the screen.

Cade.

She fumed silently. He'd done it on purpose. That was fine. The old adage, what goes around comes around, would catch him with his pants down someday.

"Right. Run with that. Ignore the pants-down part, though," she muttered. Untangling her crossed legs and nest of pillows, she slid off the little twin bed and began gathering her reports, predictions, charts and graphs from the floor. The work represented forecasts in business, advertising efficacy, projected budgets and, above all, the goals for the grand opening in a few days.

The front door slammed and heavy footfalls sounded above her.

"You can 'Cotton-eye Joe' to the kitchen for all I care,

Stompy McFee." She flipped him a one-bird salute and took all her materials to the small desk.

Ignoring the voices upstairs, she settled in to work on the guest list. She wanted a folder for each individual who had been invited, the company he or she represented, how Emma might work in potential opportunities to connect with them in future and further promote the dude ranch. This list was her last chance to keep her business. If the event flopped, if she didn't make enough contacts, she'd have nothing when she confronted Michael about his subpar work product and the company's resulting losses. If she fired him, he'd take his own failures and label them hers. He'd be able to make it appear to both her professional peers and client list that she'd become lackadaisical in her work ethic and output, and the company would suffer. She'd lose everything.

The firm knock on her bedroom door had her flinging papers again as she spun. She let out a foul curse as the door opened.

Cade stood there, two dinner plates in hand. "Thought you might enjoy a little company while you worked through dinner."

"Is it that obvious I'm skipping out on having a full-blown confrontation with you and your brothers over—" she glanced at the dinner plates "—meat loaf?" she asked, lightly.

He slipped into the room and nudged the door with his hip, pushing it shut but not bothering to latch it. "No, it was only obvious you were still working."

"You didn't have to bring dinner down." Emma set the paperwork on the edge of the desk and dropped onto the end of the bed, accepting the proffered plate. She bit her bottom lip before looking up and offering a tentative smile. "I'm glad you did, though. I appreciate the company."

"No reason to relegate yourself to your bedroom just because we've all been behaving like jerks." He settled into the desk chair, ankle resting on his opposite knee as he tucked a paper towel in the neck of his shirt. "Sorry about that, by the way. I've talked to Eli and Ty. You shouldn't meet with any more resistance."

Unwilling to check a gift horse's teeth, she opted to accept the kind gesture. It was true that part of her had holed up in the bedroom to work instead of subjecting herself to questioning and being made to feel she was nothing more than an evil, tolerated necessity. That part of her was the cowardly, vulnerable part she hated. Another part demanded she stick this out and prove to everyone, herself included, that she could, and would, do this.

"For what it's worth, I appreciate that." Emma glanced around the room, taking in the paraphernalia of a childhood spent among family and friends. "I can't imagine Eli would ever leave this." The yearning in her voice nearly choked her.

Eyes focused on his plate, Cade forked up a bite of meat loaf. "What was your childhood like, growing up in the city?"

Emma grimaced into her iced tea. "Hmm. My childhood. It was decidedly less idyllic than the one you guys seem to have experienced." She paused, considering what she'd already disclosed. "You know a bit from last night. I can add that my parents were entirely focused on their financial worth. They were more familiar with their fixed assets lists than they were with their only child."

"Why weren't they interested in you?" he asked, pushing his food around on his plate.

She sipped her tea, absently coating a throat gone dry with truth. "They were very self-important people who never wanted a child. Their birth control failed. They could have had an abortion, but they were too concerned with what their peers would say. In the end, after much discussion, they 'maintained the pregnancy' and were left with a person they aspired to mold into a miniature version of themselves. That's probably the best description."

"Any love in there?"

"Love was intangible, a waste of energy that would be better invested in making more money or further climbing the all-important social ladder. We moved several times before I left for college, always into a better, more expensive neighborhood. We also wore the right clothes, drove the right cars, comported ourselves as if we were socially superior and always utilized my parents' premium box seats at the theater. 'See and be seen in the best and by the best' was always their motto." Bitterness made her words caustic despite her best efforts. "They looked and sounded right at all times. When I was beneficial for some social function or whatever, when having a child gained them something, I was to behave as a perfect child would—be visible but silent, be polite but not appear too full of independent ideas, and, later, be a lady who would make a fine match but never a woman who might challenge society's, or her husband's, ideals. Ironically, their pursuit of perfection didn't help them live any longer."

"Not everything's as pretty as it's painted to be, is it?"

She toyed with the peas on her plate, lining them up in rows before she spoke again. "I was asked to speak at their funeral. I declined, but not for the reasons everyone suspected. It wasn't grief." Emma forced herself to meet Cade's steady gaze. "I declined because I had no idea what I could possibly say about them."

He nodded, and then set his relatively full plate on the dresser beside him, appetite seemingly lost. Dropping his foot to the floor, he leaned forward and parked his forearms on his knees. "Our mom died when we were young. She treated her boys as if the sun rose and set because of us, but our old man was…difficult? Hard? Disengaged from our lives?" He snorted. "That might be the understatement of the century. Eli left home when he was old enough and had banked a couple years of bravery. Took him fourteen years to come home. He accomplished his life goals and got the girl of his dreams in the end, so it worked out well for him."

Shifting, she leaned against the little bed's headboard. "That's great for him, but what about you and Ty? What about your dreams?"

"It's safe to say life wasn't quite so easy for us, living out here with Dad."

Emma set her own plate aside, what was left of her appetite following Cade's to parts unknown. "Okay."

She traced a finger along a hand-sewn repair to a tear in the bed's quilt. *It's safe to say life wasn't quite so easy,* he'd said, piquing Emma's curiosity. She wanted to understand what life had been like for the boy Cade had been, and how, in the end, it had shaped the man he'd become.

But admitting to her curiosity meant admitting that she was interested in him. Was she? After the way he'd treated her, with passion and heat, but also resentment that she was trying to change his way of life?

As much as it galled her, she *did* want to try to understand who he was and what made him tick.

Emma sucked in a deep breath, held it and let it out

to the count of ten. Then she forced herself to meet Cade's quiet eyes. "How did it affect *you*, Cade? How was it different for you than it was for Ty?"

His chin dropped to his chest, his voice quiet when he finally spoke. "Ty was always the baby, the one nobody expected much of because he was a kid when all this happened—Mom dying, Dad withdrawing, Eli leaving. My old man just assumed I'd take over for Eli, become the oldest son as a matter of course. I'd keep up my own responsibilities and take on his and I'd be damned grateful for it if anyone asked. There was no discussion, short of..." He shook his head. "Leave it at there was no discussion. It's sort of a weird parallel to your parents wanting you to appear perfect. There were just more of us pretending."

"How're things with you and Eli since he came home?" she asked gently.

He glanced up, his eyes darkening before he shifted and focused on the floor again. "We're working our stuff out. Takes a while." He picked at a hangnail, shoulders hunching. "I asked him to come home once."

"You asked who? Eli?"

Cade gave a short nod. "Yeah."

"Did he?"

"No. He came when Ty called after Dad died, though."

She recognized his resentment, but what shocked her was the absolute vulnerability that made the words so raw and hard to hear. "He didn't love you any less, Cade."

"Sure." He stood and held out a hand. "Done with your plate?"

She handed it to him and opened her mouth to reassure him, but he cut her off with a glare. "Don't, okay? Just don't."

"Okay," she whispered.

He opened the door, those massive shoulders still sagging and stepped around Reagan, who was standing there, hand raised to knock.

The other woman watched him go, a strange poignancy tightening the corners of her eyes. Shaking her head as if to clear it, she faced Emma. "Can I come in for a second?"

"Sure." She gestured to the chair Cade had occupied. "Have a seat."

Reagan sank down and smiled tentatively. "Everything okay?"

"Sure," she repeated. Forcing herself to let go of the last remnants of conversation with Cade, she refocused on the woman she'd so quickly come to admire for her generosity of spirit as well as her brutal efficiency. "What brings you to the dragon's lair?"

A quicksilver smile. "You're not exactly a dragon."

"Not *exactly*, but only because you never met my mother. I certainly have the appropriate genetics."

Eli's fiancée laughed. "That bad?"

"She was, yes, though she'd probably take it as a compliment." Emma curled her legs up tailor-style and scooted to rest against the headboard. "What's up?"

"I actually came down to talk to you about a possible favor." Reagan fidgeted in her chair. "I hate asking for favors."

Emma grinned. "Hit me."

"You coordinate special events."

"I've even tried to make a career of it, yes," Emma said, grinning wider.

Reagan buried her face in her hands. "I'm an idiot. Of course you have."

Emma's laughter was softer than Reagan's had been.

"What's going on, Reagan? I'm sure I can help somehow."

"Do you ever coordinate weddings?" Reagan blurted.

Emma's brows shot up. "Weddings?" Caught off guard, she struggled to pull her thoughts together. "I've done them in the past. I worked for a florist in college and did my internship with a national bridal chain's marketing department. Why?"

"I have to find a wedding coordinator. *Have to*, Emma. I'm getting married in four and a half months, and with the ranch opening, I haven't checked off a single thing on my To Do list." Reagan's shoulders slumped. "It doesn't help that I completely suck at this stuff."

"Hey," Emma said, moving to the end of the bed and gently bumping her knee against Reagan's. "You've done an amazing job here. There's nothing wrong with asking for a little help."

Bleak eyes met her own. "It's more than 'a little help,' Emma. I don't have a dress. I don't even know what kind of dress would best suit my figure. I don't have colors because I have *no freaking clue* how to determine the difference between what one bridal consultant called 'chestnut' and another called 'henna' and yet another called 'titian.'" She shoved her hands through her long hair. "*Titian*, for heaven's sake! I had to Google it. If any one of them had spoken English and just said 'rust-colored,' I'd have been fine!"

Quivering with suppressed laughter, Emma simply shook her head. "I'd be more than happy to help."

"It's not exactly 'help' I'm after." Reagan pulled her trademark ponytail down and shook out her hair. Massaging her scalp, she sighed heavily. "What would you charge to take over the whole thing? I want someone to give Eli and me a time and place to show up. I want to carry a gorgeous bouquet of seasonally appropriate flowers. I want to take my vows in front of people who received beautiful invitations that I had nothing to do with. I want to eat delicious cake someone else designed and then purchased. I want to dance to music from a live band that plays music I like. And then I want to go on a honeymoon where I can sleep and eat good food and relax, preferably where the weather's better than it will be here that time of year. Is that too much to ask?" She laughed, the sound slightly crazed. "I probably can't afford you, can I?"

Emma considered her. "I have an idea. What if we use your wedding to create a brochure for the ranch, something that promotes destination weddings?"

Reagan flopped back in the chair. "I'd *have* to have someone coordinate it, then."

"Exactly, and then you could write it off as a business expense." Emma grinned as she saw the light go on in the other woman's eyes. "We can make it all work within your budget. And my mind is already whirring. I have a few thoughts on how to showcase the venue without compromising your day." Emma grabbed a notebook, flipped to a blank sheet of paper and began jotting down possibilities, from the type of dress that would showcase the tall woman's willowy form, to possible colors, to trendy cake flavors, to the number of guests the couple planned to invite.

Reagan hopped up and pulled Emma into a huge hug. "Promise me you'll do it, that you'll handle the whole event. I don't want anyone else. I'm sure Eli will agree."

Something in Emma bloomed. She hadn't felt so necessary in ages, so important to one person's happiness. "I promise. I'll handle it all myself."

"And you'll be here, right? You won't handle it remotely, but you'll be *here*, prepared to talk me out of knocking Eli out and dragging him off for a Vegas quickie?"

A sharp burst of laughter escaped Emma at the idea of just such a thing, both participants clad in their wedding finery, the bride shoving the groom in her mobile veterinary clinic truck and leaving stunned guests in a cloud of dust. "I promise you I'll be here, Reagan. I'll even pinkie-swear, but I draw the line at blood oaths."

Reagan chuckled, then grabbed Emma by the shoulders. "Can I ask you something?"

"Another favor?" she teased.

"No." The woman's gaze bored into hers. "I know you and Cade have been together."

The blood rushed from Emma's cheeks so fast she got light-headed. "I'm sincerely sorry, but what happened is between us. I can't discuss it and would ask that you don't, either. It won't—"

"Do you care about him?" Reagan asked, abruptly interrupting Emma's rushed explanation. "I want the truth, Emma. That's all that matters to me. Not what happened or whether it will happen again. I swear to you. I only want to know if he matters to you."

"He does," Emma choked out around the fifteen-car pileup of emotion in her throat. "More than I want to either admit or deal with. Why?"

The other woman closed her eyes and breathed deeply. "I'm getting married. It's not so crazy to want my first real girlfriend ever to be happy, too, is it?"

Ignoring the gentle pang of envy that rang through her heart, Emma chose to focus on the fact that this amazing woman considered her a friend.

"No. I suppose it's not."

CADE LAY ON his bed and listened to the murmur of feminine voices next door. He'd left the bathroom door cracked, but all he could catch was a word now and again—dragon, marriage, dude ranch, brochure, budget, Eli, death, hate, help.

Was Reagan explaining how Cade had almost ruined the ranch? That Eli, with his wealth and generosity, was the only one that had been able to save the ranch from being shuttered after an outbreak of shipping fever?

Taking his older brother's handouts had almost destroyed what little pride Cade had managed to salvage throughout the whole shipping fever nightmare. Emma would find out how Cade hadn't been able to save the place without charity and his big brother's intervention.

The ulcer he believed he'd beaten started burning a hole in his gut again.

He couldn't be angry with Reagan for reaching out to Emma. She had no female friends, but was, instead, stuck out here with the men all day, every day. That had to wear on her. She had Eli, sure, but there were bound to be moments of loneliness.

He'd never been in love, but no way could someone else be a person's everything. Banking on one person for that was foolishness, anyway. That kind of investment gave a person the kind of control one should never relinquish. Ever. And as far as emotions went? The same rule existed to an exponential level. He'd done it once, banking every emotional dollar he had in Eli coming home when Cade had begged him to. His older brother had shut him down and shut him out.

He sat up, scrubbing his hands over his face. This was ridiculous, sitting here straining to catch words.

Shoving off the bed, he cursed when the frame slipped

and the headboard bumped the wall with a decisive *thump.*

Voices next door extinguished at the sound. Time suspended as he waited for a reaction, and then someone laughed, low and sultry.

Emmaline.

Reagan was a beautiful woman in her own right, but she was no Emmaline. Particularly when the latter laughed. God save him from that sound, the way it pulled at him and made him want to do inexplicable things, the way it made him feel ten feet tall when he was responsible for it.

Why doesn't she laugh more? Why is she usually so serious?

He laughed at himself. *Pot to kettle, my man.*

A soft knock at the door had him spinning around. *Emma?* "Yeah?" The word emerged gruff and gravelly from his tight throat.

Reagan stuck her head in. "Got a second?"

He tried to keep his disappointment disguised. "For you? Always."

She smiled. Somehow, she realized he'd expected a different woman at his door.

Glancing at him, her smile widened. "How you doing, Cade?"

"Fine." He waited a moment. When she didn't move, he asked, "And you?"

Her answer came across as a tad absentminded. "I'm really good. You're sure I'm not interrupting?"

He stepped out of the doorway and swept his arm wide, on open invitation to enter.

Instead of stepping inside, though, Reagan stayed where she was and stared at him. "I have a theory."

"Oh-kay…" His future sister-in-law's eyes gleamed

with a mischievous light that made Cade's hindbrain go on complete alert, his fight-or-flight instinct kicking in, and hard.

"Want to help me prove or disprove it?"

"If it'll get you to go upstairs and get a good night's sleep, my answer's yes. The stress of the opening seems to be getting to you, darlin'."

"Emma!" she shouted.

"Reagan," he all but growled. "What are you doing?"

Emma stepped out and glanced between them, clearly confused. "Yeah?"

"Do you like Cade?"

She paled. "He's been a decent, if slightly difficult, client."

"Not what I asked." One corner of Reagan's mouth kicked up. "Do you like-him, like-him, as in would you consider going out on a date with him?"

Emma's eyes widened as Cade choked. He was going to have to come up with one hell of a condolence card to send Eli because he was going to *kill* Reagan for this.

"That's enough," he said.

At the same moment, Emma spoke. "He asking?"

"Yeah, he is." Reagan glanced from one to the other. "He's taking you to Clayton to go to dinner and then dancing at Bits 'n Spurs Friday night. It's jeans-and-boots-and-a-sexy-top kind of place."

She paled. "I don't dance."

"He's excellent. He'll teach you." Reagan rounded on Cade. "Only thing you've got to figure out is where to go for dinner. Eli can give you a recommendation if you can't come up with a decent place. Cool?" Before he could answer, she nodded. "Good. Emma, I don't know what you brought in the way of clothes, so shout out if you need to borrow a top." Then she took off up the stairs muttering about men being morons.

"I actually feel sorry for Eli," Emma murmured, watching her go.

The sentiment caught Cade off guard. "Why?"

"She's going to go have some very domineering sex with him, and he'll have no idea what he did to deserve it." She grinned. "Or how to do it again." Shifting her gaze to meet his, she nodded. "I get the impression you just got railroaded. It's okay if you want to cancel this now."

He opened his mouth to do just that, but what came out was, "Be ready by six on Friday."

Stunned at his brazen stupidity, he spun on his heel, went into his room and shut the door. Standing there, he listened for her door to close. The moment the latch clicked, the second he was truly alone, he grinned.

He had a date with the woman, the *only* woman, who drove him so crazy that he was beginning to think he couldn't live without her.

10

EMMA WASN'T ENTIRELY sure what had happened to the past three days, but they'd disappeared in a rush of work.

Two days ago she'd taken the trucking company responsible for delivering the furniture to its knees. The furniture had shown up this morning, seven days ahead of schedule. That meant she'd been putting the finishing touches on the cabins, ironing and hanging curtains, arranging furniture for appeal and to maximize space.

She'd finished about an hour before dinner, giving her a chance to quietly move all of her stuff to the little one-bedroom honeymoon cabin while the family was preoccupied. It had taken a couple of clandestine trips to transfer everything, but she'd managed.

She was officially out of the house.

Reagan had looked at her funny when she'd come in for a quick meal, but the woman hadn't questioned Emma in the midst of sandwich-making chaos. Every time the brothers descended on the kitchen, they inevitably left scraps of this and pieces of that. When all was said and done, the kitchen appeared as if an F5 tornado had swept through the space. It was insane that feeding three educated, civilized men could leave such chaos in its wake.

She began cleaning up with one hand while she ate her sandwich with the other, but Reagan waved her off. "I've got this. Practice has taught me how to best manage the mess. It's something no sane woman should have to tackle until she's so smitten that it doesn't leave her with that particular expression."

"What expression?" Emma asked, grateful to set her sponge down.

"The one that wordlessly asks, 'How do these men behave in public?'" The other woman laughed. "You're smitten, yes, but not quite enough to handle cleanup."

Swamped with a strange sense of discomfort, Emma nodded. Some things she simply wasn't good at, and keeping house was one of them, particularly when that house was a home. She had no idea how to cultivate that kind of warmth, to make a room livable or to make a house the center of the family dynamic. "I envy you this," Emma said reverently.

Reagan paused in the middle of spraying the counters with 409 and looked up. "You what?"

"I…nothing."

"Seriously, Emma. You envy me what?"

She finished chewing her bite of sandwich and took a swallow of lemonade. Anything to stall. But there was only so much she could do before her mouth, dry with anxiety, was empty.

"This." She swept her hand around in a wide arc. "You have a *way* about you, an almost maternal air, that gives off a sense of security. You've made me feel so at home, so welcome. I wouldn't hesitate to dig through the fridge to get whatever I crave, or to make a sandwich at 2:00 a.m., because I'm sure you won't mind and of course there will be food. A mom never allows a house to run out of food." Eyes burning, she closed them and continued. "Usually there's nothing more than bottled water and a bad lemon in my fridge. I have a cleaning service come in because I can't manage the housework on a two-bedroom condo occupied by one constantly absent person. An interior decorator decked out my house for a magazine shoot. He did such a good job I'm afraid to put my feet on my own sofa." She opened her eyes, staring at Reagan through the faint sheen of tears. "I don't want to return to Seventy-second Avenue because it's not my *home*. Worse? I'd give anything to make it feel like *this*, but I don't have that skill. I've always lived in a house, never a home, and it just hit me how horribly lonely it really is."

Closing her eyes again, Emma willed the last bite of sandwich down. It hit bottom heavier than a lead ball. She wiped her mouth on her paper towel and cleared her throat. "I'm sorry, Reagan. Truly. I've never been mothered, and it just occurred to me that I've thrived on your nurturing." Hesitantly, she touched Reagan's arm.

Cade stomped into the kitchen. "Forgot my water bottle."

Reagan studied Emma for the briefest second before setting the sponge down. "Emma, will you grab Cade's bottle? You're nearer the fridge, and if he comes in here all filthy after we just cleaned up, I'll kill him."

"Sure." She moved toward the refrigerator.

"I'll grab the stuff so we can make cookies."

Emma stumbled. "Cookies?" she called in a total panic.

But Reagan didn't answer, just lifted a hand in acknowledgment and skipped down the stairs to the basement.

"What's in the basement that's necessary to make cookies?" Emma demanded of Cade.

He shrugged. "Chocolate chips are always in the freezer, so I'd imagine that's what she's after. Maybe butter since we buy in bulk and it keeps longer if it's frozen. Why?"

She wanted to answer, but the words wouldn't come.

"Emma?"

"Cookies," she wheezed. "I've never made cookies. Hell, I can't cook. What is she thinking?"

Cade faced her, his brow creasing. "It's just chocolate chip cookies, Emma. Maybe Ranger cookies if she brings up the coconut, too." Emma saw the moment he registered just how foreign to her this was, how alien his upbringing had been to hers. "Wait. Your mom never made cookies with you?"

"My mom wasn't the mothering type, Cade. I told you, I had nannies." She hated, *hated*, the fact she couldn't make that statement without her voice wavering. But this whole experience, from the moment Michael had given her the file until now, had spun her in circle after circle until she was dizzy with emotion.

The line between his brows deepened. "Right, but I thought... Your nannies didn't do stuff with you?"

"They didn't usually last that long. I never even saw the cook make a meal."

Cade moved in close, his movements slow and deliberate, his voice soft. "What did you eat?"

"Whatever I was told to eat."

"You didn't rebel if they put broccoli on your plate?"

"No!" she nearly shouted. "No." Quieter. "I ate what I was served, alone more often than not, and always with the right utensils. I ate in the kitchen so as not to disturb my parents' meal, and the cook refused to eat with me. If I complained, I was sent to bed with an empty stomach.

So, no, I don't know how to make *cookies*." Her voice broke, surprising her.

"Oh, Emma."

He crossed to her in three long strides and pulled her into his embrace, surrounding her with the smell of hot cotton and sunshine, and she completely fell apart.

He held her as she cried, rocking her and whispering wordlessly into her hair, his hands soothing her with tender touches while his arms offered sanctuary. Minutes later, she understood what he was whispering.

"I've got you, baby," he said, over and over into the hair at the crown of her head.

Collecting herself, she stepped out of his embrace and wiped her face. "I apologize. I had no business crying on you." *And over* cookies, she realized, mortified. Her mother was likely spinning in her grave so hard she was pulling three g's.

"You had every right to cry, honey." Cade's tone was melted chocolate poured over honed steel, a sharp edge dividing his tone into equal parts compassion and ferocity. "Don't ever apologize for tears shed over a wrong done you."

"It's so long past, Cade. Crying isn't going to change what was any more than it will affect what is." She went to the sink and splashed cold water on her face. "If you'll give me a moment, I'll get you the bill of lading for the furniture delivery."

"Furniture doesn't arrive for another couple of days."

"It arrived this morning, actually." She offered a small, unsteady smile. "I got on the phone two days ago and had the company's ass for breakfast."

He shook his head and chuckled. "I'm learning to never underestimate you, Ms. Graystone."

"Wise man, Mr. Covington," she responded, forcibly

settling her world on its axis once again and giving it a mental nudge to set it spinning.

He gave a single dip of his chin. "I'm at cabin eleven. Bring that bill of lading down when you're done here." He was halfway across the living room before he stopped and gave her his profile. "Five bucks says your cookies kick ass." And then he was gone.

A genuine smile stole across her face.

Wouldn't that *be something?*

CADE HUNG THE last shutter on the final cabin before slipping his hammer into the loop on his tool belt. He pulled up his shirt and wiped his face, neck and chest before tossing the tee into his tool bag. The area was well lit by new arena lights, casting long shadows even though it was way past dark. He climbed down the ladder and stepped twenty or so feet away from the cabin to take in the completed job. A sense of fierce satisfaction wound through him, and he wondered idly, as he dug a cookie out of the cooler, if Emma had experienced the same sense after her first—very successful—attempt at cookies.

Since he was the last one working tonight, Cade was left putting away all the tools before heading to the barn to shut out the lights. His horse, Ziggy, nickered, demanding attention. Glancing around a little guiltily, he went to the fridge in the tack room and grabbed a can of Coke. Taking it to Ziggy's stall, he opened the can and set it on the wide sill of the stall door. The horse picked up the can and tilted his head back, spilling as much of the soft drink as he managed to get down his throat before dropping the can and tossing his head. If a horse could express glee, Ziggy's face was radiant with it. The

Coke was their little secret—Ziggy was a sugar addict and Cade was his supplier. Whatever. It clearly worked.

Cade laughed as the horse flapped his lips for more. "Nope. You're cut off at one can, my friend. You're far too close to the edge as it is. What will we do if you go over? Your loyalty could be compromised entirely, and for what? A single twelve-ounce fix? You'll hate yourself in the morning." The horse snorted and pawed at the stall door, and Cade lifted his brows. "See? You've already been reduced to begging for your next hit. Where's your pride, man? And when will you realize one hit is never enough? We'll fight this together. I promise."

Cade bent down and swept up the discarded can, chuckling. The recycle bin was almost full. He'd have to empty it tomorrow—the day of his date with Emma. Maybe he and Emma could leave a little early so he could dispose of the recyclables at the depot in Clayton. Might bring in a couple hundred bucks.

He began flipping heavy switches. The barn went dark first, followed by the arena and then the landscape lighting. That's when he noticed one of the cabins was completely lit up.

It would have been easiest just to cut the power to all the cabins and check it out tomorrow, but if there happened to be a short or if one of his brothers happened to still be working... But he'd watched them head inside at least an hour earlier.

"Folks have to learn to switch lights off. Utility bills are going to leave us eating dandelion soup and boiling river water for drinking." He yanked his hat off his head and slapped it against his thigh as he walked. A decidedly feminine shadow moved by the window, her form backlit against the curtain. *Emma.*

"What are you up to, Ms. Graystone?" he murmured.

Music sounded faintly through the door. Not just any music, either. It was the Tyler Farr album he'd had in his truck. He wasn't sure if she'd lifted it from him or had downloaded it from somewhere. But she was clearly singing along, her voice low and sultry and just off tune enough to be positively endearing. She was also dancing.

He moved closer to the window, shifting so he could see through the split in the shades. This was definitely not the kind of dancing they'd be doing tomorrow night. These were dangerous moves, the kind that whipped a man into a frenzy right before they rendered him a complete fool. He watched those hips sway, found himself seduced by the way they swiveled and thrust with the music, and admitted to himself it wouldn't be so horrible to be a fool.

Cade grinned as he adjusted his enthusiastic erection. Man alive, that woman could *move*. He couldn't wait to get her on the dance floor.

She spun by the window and something else inside caught his attention. His grin was wiped away as if it had never been. Emma wasn't working in the cabin. *She'd moved in.*

Damn if he was going to let that stand. She was a guest in their house, a guest in *his* house, and she wasn't staying in a cabin. This way she'd be out of reach, too far away from him.

He wanted to be close in case she needed him for any reason. He wanted to hear her getting ready for bed. Wanted to hear her get up in the morning. Craved listening to her humming as she brushed her teeth. To be reassured that she was still there, that she hadn't disappeared into the night, hadn't left him with complicated memories and unresolved tomorrows.

He stepped to the door to knock and a hard hand gripped his fist. "I wouldn't."

Cade whipped around, his other hand already fisted and headed toward the source of the voice.

The dark shadow ducked and yanked on his dominant hand at the same time, pulling Cade off-balance. "Cut it out, little brother."

Eli.

"Thanks for the reminder on the official rank and order. What are you doing out here?" Cade asked, panting from a combination of adrenaline and…more adrenaline.

"Came out here to ask you the same thing. Saw all the lights go out but you never made it to the house. Wanted to make sure you didn't forget your way home."

"Unless you decided to wear ruby slippers, clicked your heels together, whispered 'There's no place like home' and dropped the house on some unsuspecting soul somewhere else, I'm good, thanks." Cade pulled his hand free of Eli's grip with a bit of force. Wouldn't have been necessary if Eli had simply let go, but in typical big-brother fashion, he hadn't.

The guy had been nowhere in sight when Cade had needed him most, and now he was trying to slip into the authoritative role? Life didn't work that way. Not as far as Cade was concerned, anyhow. He'd covered for Eli for years, and not once had the sacrifice been acknowledged. Not by anyone, but especially not by Eli.

"Thickheaded or not, you're not stupid, Cade. When I said 'don't forget your way home,' you know I was telling you to put one foot in front of the other and get to bed." Eli's terse tone said he expected no argument.

Good thing I enjoy keeping people on their toes, amending expectations now and again. Before he could snipe a reply, Eli was talking again. *Damn lawyer.* But Emma's name grabbed his attention.

"Keep your distance where Emma's concerned. First, she works for us. Second, from my own conversations with her and more intimate conversations she's had with Reagan that Emma has a lot riding on this event. And third? Might be the toughest to hear, but it's also the most relevant as it relates to you. You're your own man, Cade. You don't need her to validate your worth."

"I'm going to walk away from you and pretend for both our sakes that you did *not* just say that to me." Cade stepped away from the cabin, eyes on Eli's shadowy figure. He made it several feet before spinning on his heel and stalking away.

The crunch of Eli's boots behind him said this wasn't over.

Fan-freaking-tastic. Just what I need. An "intervention" from the big brother that never was. Swinging around, he glared at Eli through the darkness. "Look—" he started, but Eli cut him off.

"I want to talk to you."

"You said your piece. And frankly? I don't appreciate you ordering me to mind myself where she's concerned. It was your wife who set us up on tomorrow night's date." Eli barely managed to swallow his surprise, and Cade grinned. "Didn't tell you that part, huh? You might want to get your facts sorted before you come out here to jump my ass, *brother.*"

Once again, Eli grabbed him and yanked him around. "Stop it."

"Stop. What." The hard bite to each word should have been warning enough.

"I… That is, I wanted to say…" Eli let go of Cade and moved out of reach. "I've been home for almost a year, yet for every two steps forward, we find ourselves set back at least one."

Cade tucked his thumbs in his pocket and snorted. "This isn't a dance, Eli."

"Yeah, well, if it were, I'd always be missing the beat and stepping on your toes." Eli raised his hands and scrubbed them through his hair. "What do I have to do to fix this, Cade? What's it going to take to make this right between us?"

Cade shrugged, uncomfortable enough to find himself taking up the defensive. "I'm glad you're home, but it doesn't change the fact you left us, me and Ty, to deal with the old man. Hit me up in a little over a decade and see where we're at then." He started toward the house again, throat tight and steps slow as he waited for Eli to deliver some parting shot, but it never came. Slowing to a stop, he waited, but no footsteps sounded behind him. And that, the permission to walk away—the permission he'd lacked all his life—sprang the lock on Cade's bitterness.

He turned, his breath coming faster, his hands clenching and unclenching. "You were gone for fourteen years, Eli. You don't get to waltz off to chase *your* dreams, to live *your* life, and then come back here to claim *your* happily ever after without consequences. You left me!" he shouted. "You left me to be the son Dad had to settle for because his oldest took off. Nothing I did was ever good enough, nothing I said was ever smart enough, no suggestion I made was ever man enough. I was trying to be you *and* me, trying to protect Tyson from the brunt of Dad's anger, and you know what? I couldn't. The most I could do was put myself in his way."

"Did he hit you?" Eli asked quietly.

Eli stepped toward him, but Cade backed away. "I

asked you to come home, Eli. I begged you. I didn't want him beating on Tyson, didn't want him hurting the kid. And you were crystal clear when you said to me that you'd made your life in Austin, that there was nothing left here for you to come back to."

Eli's breath sawed in and out, and his voice ripped through the darkness. "I didn't know. I swear to God, Caden, I didn't know."

"I wanted you to save us," he said in a voice so broken he hardly recognized it as his own.

"I would have. I give you my word, I would have come home."

"You did. For him. At least I managed to spare him the most of it." Rubbing his chest, Cade stepped farther away. "It's finished, Eli. It's finished and Dad's dead. But there are still moments when I resent the hell out of the fact you ended up getting everything you wanted."

"What do you want from me? What can I do to—"

"Nothing," Cade said, fighting to keep himself from falling apart. "There's nothing you can do."

"We have a chance here, Cade. *You* have a chance. Let me make this right. Let me help you realize your dreams."

"Don't you get it?" he asked so quietly the crickets nearly drowned out his words, only the breeze carrying his words to his brother. He tipped his chin up and stared at the millions of stars overhead. *How many wishes did I make growing up? How often did I wish for a miracle? How many nights did I wish Eli would show up and save them? Too many to count.* He huffed out a broken laugh. "It was never my lot in life to wish or dream, only to survive. And now? I can't do anything more than that. It'll have to be enough."

Eli started to respond, but Cade shook his head,

turned and strode to the house with a swift but measured pace. He wouldn't run. The only thing to chase him were the ghosts of what might have been, and they'd dogged his heels so long he knew he wasn't fast enough to get away.

As in every other aspect of life, he wasn't enough.

11

DESPITE THE MUSIC, Emma had heard the deep, familiar voices outside her door. Not wanting a confrontation with Cade over moving out of the house without his almighty consent, she'd sneaked to a side window. The tall window would open enough to let her slip the screen off, crawl out and disappear into the night unnoticed. Yeah, he'd figure it out and give her hell, but that was fine. That would happen later, and she'd surely be more prepared *later*.

Slipping her hands behind the curtains, she flipped the window latch and pulled it up as gently as she could, pulling harder as it went higher. And then it got stuck. She couldn't get it to budge, neither up *nor* down, and cursing it hadn't made a bit of difference. It was well and truly wedged in place. A hard yank and the bottom of the screen popped off. Emma caught it seconds before the whole screen flopped—loudly—onto the ground.

"Note to self," she whispered, words hard-edged. "Check all cabin windows for functional emergency egress *before* escape proves necessary."

With a little contortionist-like maneuvering, she managed to squat in front of the almost floor-to-ceiling window, the screen's frame held gently in her palms. She hoped the conversation between the men was a short one. If it wasn't? If her muscles cramped? The screen would crash. Discovery loomed, imminent, immense and inevitable.

Busy contemplating the probability that one could, in fact, die of mortification, it took her a moment to realize the conversation had stopped with the sound of skin hitting skin. Hard. Then heavy breathing.

"Cut it out, little brother." *Eli.*

"Thanks for the reminder on the official rank and order." *Cade.* "What are you doing out here?"

"Came out here to ask you the same thing. All the lights went out but you never made it to the house. Wanted to make sure you didn't lose your way."

"Unless you decided to wear ruby slippers, clicked your heels together, whispered 'There's no place like home' and dropped the house on some unsuspecting soul somewhere else, I'm good, thanks." *Cade.* That voice— normally smooth, now gravelly with emotion—carried across the night air. It held in it a whispered promise of violence, a rough assertion to Eli that he should get out of Cade's personal space. There was nothing ambiguous or benign in the statement or, apparently, between the brothers.

Eli had clearly come down to check up on Cade and stage a little intervention, which meant he had to have suspected his younger brother would deviate from the straight line that ran from barn to house. And Emma was right in between the two buildings, representing that deviation. Cade had been at her door.

He'd come to her.

Her stomach did an involuntary gymnastics routine. She sucked in a breath. Cade wasn't a man to waste words, and Emma wasn't stupid. He'd have laid things out in black-and-white, explained how things between them were going to go. She'd have argued, negotiating the finer points as a matter of self-respect, and he'd have ended up in her bed tonight. That he'd shown up meant he wanted her. It was only a small skip and a hop from his wanting her to her mattering to him, and that was likely the reason he sounded so irritated at having been caught sneaking around by none other than Eli.

"What are you, Graystone? Fourteen? Act like a woman, for heaven's sake," she muttered. Stuck as she was, still half crouched, half squatting with a large window screen in her hands and hiding half behind the curtains, she realized she had two choices—if Cade had, indeed, come to her, she could set the screen down, thus announcing her presence before opening the front door as a normal person would. Or she could continue as she was and eavesdrop on a conversation she surely wasn't meant to hear. Her cheeks heated with humiliation. Cade deserved better than this from her.

Emma opened her mouth to announce her presence when she heard retreating footsteps. The conversation must have wrapped up as she held her internal ethics summit. So much for opening the door and being the one to ride to her cowboy's rescue.

Her cowboy. She grinned. Juvenile, yes. Impossible, even more so. Still, she liked the way that sounded. Standing, she let the screen slide through her hands. It hit the ground just as Cade's voice, tormented with embattled senses of ageless despair and immediate fury, tore across the still night air and obliterated the distance between Eli and him.

He shouted at his older brother, his voice—and her heart—breaking over the things he'd obviously longed to say to Eli for more than a decade. Words that revealed a bond that had been broken by one's dreams and another's desperation. And none of it mattered but that Cade had suffered, still suffered, from a history neither he, nor the brother he held responsible, could change.

A fierce desire to protect him rose in her, to pull him close and put herself between him and that history, to somehow change or erase the things that had hurt him and still haunted him. But life didn't offer do-overs.

The hardships Cade laid bare were paired with the isolation that had followed him into adulthood, and they combined to break her. Emma wrapped her arms around herself and moved toward the front door as if pulled by some invisible rope, some intangible *thing* she didn't understand. All she understood right then was that she had to get to Cade.

She pulled the front door open to find nothing but silence and a sky full of millions of stars—any of which might have been those wished on by the boy Cade had been.

CADE STORMED THROUGH the house, boots on, and went straight to his room. He wasn't in the mood to play the role of perfect middle child, the brother who fell in line with the returning elder brother's brilliant plans to save the day and be grateful for the handouts. Screw. That.

Stripping down to his boxers, he pulled on a pair of nylon training pants and sneakers, grabbed a towel and climbed up the stairs. Ignoring Reagan's curious stare, he grabbed a bottle of water from the fridge and wordlessly brushed by both Tyson and Eli on his way to the front door.

Tyson started to say something, but Eli cut him off with a low comment.

"Stay the hell out of this, Ty," Cade barked. "And you keep your damn mouth shut, Eli."

He slammed out of the house and broke into a jog, heading to the barn. Passing Emma's cabin, he noticed that one of the screens had come off the window and almost stopped to fix it, but it could wait until tomorrow. Right now he needed to unleash some of the violence surfing his temper's high tide.

He opened the barn's breaker box and flipped the appropriate switch, lighting up the massive building. Horses shuffled and snorted in protest, some sticking their heads over stall doors to figure out what the late-night fuss was about. Unimpressed when Cade threw his hat Frisbee-style across the alley and bounced it off a vacant stall, most of them withdrew.

Cade went into the tack room and hoisted the aged canvas punching bag over his shoulder. He pulled down the large hanging scales and hung the punching bag. He should have brought the tape, wrapped his hands and taken care of his body, but the truth was he didn't care. He let loose.

Punches flew, the solid thud of each impact muffled in the barn's wide alleyway. The bag swung wildly. Support chains creaked in protest as they took the brunt of each blow and brought the bag back for more. One knuckle split, then another. He just kept whaling on the bag with everything he had.

Sweat ran into his face and blinded him. He began to crave the water he'd brought with him, but his rage, his raw hurt, ran too hot to stop. Not yet. God save him, maybe not ever.

"Cade."

The soft entreaty had him whipping around, the bag

swinging into him and knocking him forward. Toward the voice. Toward— "Emma."

She wore cowboy boots with a short, silky sundress that flowed around her as she walked toward him with slow deliberation. Something in her seemed off, troubled even, when she paused.

"You left." The accusation slipped out between his heavy breaths. She was close, too close.

"I've been within your reach since the moment we met in Amarillo. You've only had to reach out, Cade. Then…and now."

He started for her with no idea what he'd do when he got there.

She did the same, yet her movements were filled with purpose.

They met in the middle, her musky, sultry-as-sin smell hitting him a second before his mouth closed over hers in an unspoken demand that she answer in kind. It was a demand she met with her own counterclaim, one that required he give himself to her in equal measure. Tongues tangled together with something far more raw than even their first wild night.

Arms wrapped around bodies. She slid one of her legs up the outside of his thigh. He gripped her behind the knee and pulled that leg higher, settling his rock-hard erection against her cleft and thrusting, short erratic movements that drew soft sounds of encouragement from her.

Her nails scraped his scalp as she raked her fingers through his sweaty hair.

He craved this, this wild, uncontrolled passion, this silent affirmation. She'd come to him. His chest swelled, his heart thundering even harder. She wanted him, needed this from him. Seeking him out for a communion of bodies, for a connection. She craved him. Only him. For her, he was enough.

Tearing his mouth away from hers, he buried his face in the crook of her neck and breathed her in.

Her fingers tightened in his hair. "Don't slow down. I want you, Cade. Only you."

The echo of his thoughts broke the last of his hold on his sanity. He bent his knees, wrapped his arms around her and lifted. "Legs around my waist."

She complied even as she hauled his face up and reclaimed his mouth, her tongue mimicking the sexual thrust and retreat he hungered for.

Only from her.

Raw, aching hunger made him clumsy as he stumbled forward. He held her up against the tack room door and let his weight follow. He took her mouth again as he worked his hands under her dress.

No panties. Nothing but skin.

Cade groaned, his hips driving forward so hard the head of his cock breached her sex through the fabric of his workout pants.

She moaned, reaching between them to sweep a thumb over the head.

That touch, firm and demanding, had him yanking his pants down. "I don't have a condom." He leaned forward and nipped her ear.

"I've got it covered." She mimicked his action, but she bit him harder.

And he loved it.

"Now stop talking," she whispered before licking the sting of her bite.

Cade widened his stance, positioned himself and drove forward, sheathing himself. He buried his face in her neck again, muffling his shout of pleasure against her sweat-slicked skin.

She gripped his shoulders and tightened her legs, riding him just as hard as he drove into her.

Their coupling was fast, far faster than he wanted it to be, but just as fast as he needed it. The tack room door rattled violently as he loved her well. He filled her, withdrew, and filled her again, setting a relentless pace and insistent on delivering unquestionable pleasure.

Emma took everything he gave and demanded more, whispering encouragement with language he'd never considered she might use. It was a wicked side he hadn't anticipated, and it was the spark that fanned the flames of his desire into an inferno. The burn started at the base of his spine and spread as if driven by relentless spring winds over parched grasslands. Orgasm imminent, he changed the angle of his thrusts to ensure Emma received more than enough stimulation to drive her insane.

Wrapping her arms around his neck and putting her mouth to his ear, she upped the dirty talk between pants and small mewls of pleasure.

He shifted a finite amount, finding her spot.

Finally, she came apart in his arms. She shook with the power of her release, her walls tightening around him until he couldn't hold out any longer.

Cade let go, biting his lip to keep as quiet as he could. His orgasm seemed to go on and on until he shook as hard as she did. He took her down with him to the sawdust-covered ground.

"Holy hell," he panted. "You come out here to seduce me or kill me?"

"You're still breathing," she answered, her own breath just as irregular.

"If this is what I get for working late nights, I'll leave

you my schedule for every night of the next six weeks so you know where to find me."

She laughed, her breath soft and cool against his heated skin. She shifted in his lap, curling up and laying her head against his shoulder. "Spend the night with me."

He languidly stroked a hand up and down her spine. "I'd prefer you spend the night with *me*. That way when you get up in the morning and come out of the main house, there won't be talk, since no one's aware you've moved into the cabin except…me." And Eli, but he refrained from adding that little tidbit, the knowledge not sitting well with him that he'd have to explain *how* Eli knew. When she stiffened slightly, he pressed on. "I want tonight with you, Emma. A whole night with you in my arms, your body under mine." When she didn't immediately answer and she definitely didn't relax, he pressed harder. "Please, Emma. Give me tonight."

Silence hung heavy, and Cade's heart constricted. He had to have tonight because she'd be leaving him in a week. He'd forgotten. In the midst of finding such an enormous and unexpected measure of happiness, he'd set aside the fact it was temporary. For the first time in his life, he didn't want temporary. He wanted a chance. He wanted the opportunity to convince her to stay with him beyond the terms of her contract.

But above all? He wanted her to want him, to need him, the same way he wanted and needed her.

She drew a breath.

"Okay."

12

EMMA LAY IN Cade's bed and watched him, still wet from the shower, as he pulled clothes out of the dresser. He was aware she watched him and acted with absolutely zero inhibitions. It made her want to pinch his—very fine—butt. She refrained. Barely.

Dressed, he sat on the edge of the bed and smiled when she couldn't stop a jaw-cracking yawn. "You should get a little more rest, sweetheart."

Sweetheart. He'd called her that last night. She was still grinning, may have never stopped. "You're just trying to keep me from going to the cabin."

"Maybe." He traced his thumb over her kiss-swollen lips. "I like seeing you here, pale skin barely covered by sheets I'm partially responsible for rumpling, lips red and a little swollen from my kisses, the faint flush of annoyance creeping up your neck, your hair sticking out like a hedgehog's."

A surprised laugh escaped. "You had me right up to the 'hedgehog' comment."

Cade waggled his brows. "Maybe I have a thing for hedgehogs. Stranger things have happened to folks stranded out here in the wilderness."

"Still, a hedgehog?" she said, reaching up to run her fingers through the lock of hair that had fallen over his forehead.

Cupping her face, he leaned forward and kissed her with a tenderness she wasn't prepared for. His tongue teased her lips and, when she opened to him on a sigh, a deep sound of contentment echoed in his chest. He stroked her jaw, the smoothness of her skin so different from the rough pad of his thumb. That difference represented just one of the multitude of differences between them, differences that, even in morning's early light, failed to matter to her. What mattered was this moment, this man and the fact he'd broken through walls she'd believed impenetrable.

He was the one to end the kiss, resting on his knees and scrutinizing her. Then his eyes flared and something akin to both terror and marvel passed over his face.

She propped herself on one elbow. "What?"

He shook his head and continued to stare.

"Stubborn man. What just went through your mind?"

Cade rubbed his lips carefully, seeming to weigh his words.

She waited.

He dropped his gaze before speaking. "My dad worshipped the ground my mother walked on. I don't remember much about their marriage because, honestly, that kind of love was just normal. It was all I knew. Then he lost her."

Emma took his hand and twined their fingers together, resting them against the sheets. "You all lost her, not just your dad."

"It was different for him. He considered his loss somehow greater than ours." He shrugged. "It was the first anniversary of her passing that he got stinkin' drunk, raged about how he wished he'd never loved her, wished he hadn't given his heart to her and let her take it to the grave when she left him. He cursed her that night, screaming at the night sky. I was just a boy."

She squeezed his hand. "Who was never allowed to grieve."

"Point is, all I heard was that love would screw you if it got the chance. Owe it a dime and it'd take your dollar without bothering to make change. You'd always lose more than you invested—you'd always come up short."

Her heart skipped a beat.

He looked up, those just-blue eyes meeting hers, piercing her straight to the very center of who she was and compelling her to answer.

"My parents didn't teach me anything about love. Everything I learned came from friends' families and things I overheard. It confused me as a kid." She tried to smile to soften the hard truth, but her lips only twitched. "I developed a much more universal concept of love as I grew up and watched friends fall in love, compared that to Hollywood's version and snuck the occasional romance novel into the house." Her chin lifted a fraction so she could face him head-on.

He still sat quietly. Staring at her.

Her heart skipped another beat.

"Funny," he said softly, "that two people with such screwed-up ideas about love should end up here."

"Could be." The words carried on a breath.

"If we're being honest?"

She nodded carefully, her eyes never leaving his.

He hesitated.

Her heart almost stopped.

"I believe I've fallen for you, Ms. Graystone, and it scares the ever-loving hell out of me. It goes against everything I was raised to believe, punches every panic button I have and should make me want to hop on my horse and head for the hills." His gaze dropped to their hands. That thumb, roughened by hard labor, stroked hers. "I don't want to run."

Forcing herself to sit up, she retrieved her hand so she could take his face and turn that beautiful gaze her way. "Ironic, isn't it, that I was raised to believe business was more important than people? Then I met you. Everything I thought I knew was flipped on its ear. My business is on the verge of collapse." He inhaled sharply, making his cheeks move beneath her hands. She tightened her grip, wouldn't let him look away. "And I've never been happier." His eyes widened as she moved in, her lips brushing his. "It seems inevitable, Mr. Covington, that I've fallen for you, too."

He closed his eyes, their lips still touching. "Say it. Truly say it."

"I love you, Cade Covington."

He brushed a whisper-soft kiss over her lips. "Then I suppose I can get on with the day's chores."

"Not before your reciprocate."

"You have my heart, Ms. Graystone, and have branded my soul. If that's not love, I have no idea what is." Brushing her hair aside, he kissed her forehead.

Emma was almost afraid to ask, but the way her organized mind worked, she had to know. "Where do we go from here?"

"Wherever we want, I suppose." He opened his eyes and stared at her from only a few inches away. "Wherever *you* want."

She started, pulling away and breaking contact. "You'd never be happy in New York."

"I'm not sure you'd be happy here." Calm and stoic, that was Cade.

"True."

"'Wherever we want' doesn't require an immediate answer, baby." He pressed her shoulders to the bed, following her down and caging her in his arms. "We'll decide together. Right now? I have to get my butt to work or I'm going to do something I've never done before."

"And that is?"

"Spend a lazy morning in bed with a woman, *my* woman, and work up a sweat."

"Doesn't sound terribly lazy," she said, her eyes fluttering closed.

"I'd take a while to make you sweat."

Heat bloomed between her legs and she grinned. "I doubt it."

A quick kiss and he stood. "Then I'd best get going. There's a ton to accomplish today, but you can afford a couple more hours of sleep before you have to get up. Rest. I'll come get you before ten."

She watched him go, his masculine swagger tempered by a lighter step than any she'd ever seen him exhibit. "I love you," she said so softly he shouldn't have heard her.

Still, he paused at the door and glanced over his shoulder. "Damn right you do."

Then he was gone, leaving her laughing in his wake as she snuggled under the covers. The last thing she'd expected to find in New Mexico had been the first thing she'd encountered.

Love.

With all its complications, every single risk and the very real chance she'd face personal fallout from her business partner, Emma was certain she'd found love.

WHEN SHE WAKENED AGAIN, the clock read 10:57 a.m. Obviously Cade hadn't returned for her as promised. The first twinge of doubt made her shoulders tighten uncomfortably.

"It's nothing," she said, repeating the two inadequate words of solace over and over as she showered and redressed.

But as reality set in, she started to appreciate how much she'd set herself up for heartbreak. She was leaving in a few days. His place was here, and hers was in New York. Her business—a business she was about to lose if she wasn't careful, if she didn't maximize every contact that had been invited to the ranch's inaugural event—had been the center of her life for so long. She might love Cade, but she'd still have to leave him, still have to go back to the life she'd created. Heartbreaking as it was, love wouldn't pay the bills.

She headed upstairs to search out Reagan.

The other woman was in the office fussing over her billing program and cussing a blue streak as she fought with the ranch's miserable internet connection.

"Hey. Mind if I come in?"

Reagan looked up. "If you would do that thing you did last week where you laid your hands on the computer, put your cell phone on the freaking desk, created your own hot spot and sent my inventory orders, I'd declare you a saint and set up a shrine to you in that corner," she said, jerking a thumb over her shoulder.

Emma laughed. "Glad to if you promise you'll help me figure out what to wear tonight." Butterflies fluttered behind her belly button with incredible fervor for such delicate creatures.

The taller woman swiveled her chair left and right, considering. Then she nodded. "I can definitely help.

He'll take you to dinner before you head to Bits 'n Spurs for some dancing. If you don't dress down, you're going to look out of place."

"I *am* out of place. That's not enough to keep me from going tonight, though." Emma realized what she had in Cade, realized that he was an amazing man. He was just a bit rough around the edges. But that was a huge part of his appeal—his body, his voice, his eyes, his laugh, the way his hands could touch her and make her believe she was the only woman in the world, the way he could sing a few notes and steal her heart…

She shook her head, fighting for clarity. "But whatever this thing with him is, it can't go any further than this temporary, insane fling." She fisted her hair and pulled, her wide eyes seeking Reagan's compassionate ones. "I've fallen for him, and that makes him far too dangerous to my business and my life in Manhattan. It's going to suck leaving him." Emma crossed her arms, gripping her elbows. "Maybe we should put the brakes on tonight's date. It will only complicate things further, and the last thing Cade or I want is complication."

"No." The vehemence in the one word was as effective as a verbal slap. "I swear, you two are so stubborn you wouldn't recognize opportunity if it showed up on your doorstep with a calling card." She pushed out of her chair and stormed out the door and down the hall. "C'mon."

Emma followed Reagan into the bedroom she shared with Eli.

Regan was already in the small closet, grabbing clothes off hangers. She spun and thrust a pair of jeans into Emma's arms. "Put these on. I want to see the jeans on you before I pick a top. And put on your boots."

Moving as if she was on a version of *What Not to*

Wear—"East Coast Metro Meets Wild West Chic," she accepted the pants and started for the bathroom.

"Right here, Emma. I'm not chancing you going out the window."

Oh, yeah. She knew about last night. Damn if Emma was going to ask about it, though. She wasn't about to get into a conversation about Cade's past. It would be all too easy to sell her business and move out here on a hope and a prayer where that man was concerned. He was her ultimate weakness, and she didn't do weak. But... "I don't have any underwear."

Reagan barked out a laugh and pulled out a brand-new package of thongs. "You learn to stock up on the practicalities with Covington men. Eli can be a little... destructive."

With an amused chuckle, she accepted the new underwear. She pulled off her sundress and shimmied into the jeans. "Damn, they're tight."

"Breathing isn't required or even expected when your man takes you out on the town. Not out here." Reagan grinned. "Wow. I thought you were curvier than I am, but damn. What I'd give to have an ass like that."

Emma blushed and half laughed, half wheezed out her response. "Pilates."

Reagan shifted and slapped her own ass. "Saddle butt."

They laughed as if they'd been friends for ages instead of a week, but time didn't matter. Emma was simply grateful to have found a woman to commiserate with.

CADE LEFT EARLY in order to allow Emma to get a little more sleep. She'd been exhausted. So was he, but that didn't matter. No matter how late he'd been up pleasuring her body and seeking his own from hers, chores still had to be done. There was no such thing as a "nookie pass" out here.

He skipped down the porch stairs, muscles fluid, gait almost languid. Male pride made him want to pound his chest. He snorted at his asinine inclinations. Truly, though, the look on her face would stay with him all day, perhaps longer.

He'd lost his heart, and that meant it wouldn't be long before he made a special trip to Albuquerque to locate the best jeweler the city could offer. He wanted to offer her something big enough to matter but small enough to keep from being ostentatious. Classic, she'd once called herself. That's what she deserved. Something classic.

Cade checked himself. *What was he doing?*

He had to get away from thoughts of forever, let his heart and nerves settle, before he could make a logical decision about how and when things should go down. She'd shown him last night that he was everything she desired, and the results had blown his heart wide-open. But he couldn't trust that his head was screwed on straight, either.

Softly singing the latest Luke Bryan song, he forced himself to focus on their incoming guests. That strangers were arriving in a week made him want to puke. He'd really hoped he'd get over that sensation, but no. Not even close. He'd be opening his home, his private life, his *way of life*, to a bunch of people willing to pay for the "experience."

And maybe that was what irked him most. They'd be cared for, cooked for, their horses tended. They'd get an idyllic representation of ranch life. They wouldn't build fence, butcher their own beef, mend tack, deal with sick animals or fret because they were out of milk and it was fifty-four miles to the closest town to get more.

They wouldn't truly be living the life, but rather getting a postcard image of being a cowboy.

The idea of having kids at the ranch, instilling in them the morals and values this way of life demanded, appealed to Cade. He grinned. If it killed him, he was going to get programs going for the little kids, particularly goat roping and sheep riding. They'd eat it up, and *that* would nearly make it all worth it for him.

He was still grinning when he noticed Emma's cabin window was open. He remembered jogging past the window last night and seeing it open. Grabbing his master key, he went to the door only to find it unlocked. It hit him harder than he expected that she'd planned to come back here, that she hadn't come to him with the intent of staying with him.

"Don't be a drama queen," he said softly. "She asked you to spend the night with her, Covington. You talked her into coming with you instead."

A gentle push opened the cabin door, and he stepped inside. The window had been open all night, and the morning breeze had scattered file folders and paper from the side table she'd been using as a desk all over the floor. The blue notebook he'd rarely seen her without now had a green counterpart. Could be her next project. That led to thoughts of her leaving and the last of his light mood evaporated.

She couldn't just pick up and go, couldn't abandon him after claiming to love him. Neither life nor love worked that way.

He moved closer to the table and saw that the spine on the unfamiliar folder had been labeled "Covington Amendments." The amendments must have been what she'd talked to the family about when he'd gone on his hard ride. Curiosity gripped him and he reached for the folder, but the wind gusted and scattered more papers.

Moving to the window, he muscled it down. *Why had she taken the screen off?* Rubbing his chest as anxiety settled in, he tried to shake it off. He'd just go outside to put the screen on after he cleaned up here a little. Again, no big deal.

Returning to the table, he began picking up papers, generally doing his best to ignore the ledger sheets with their linear, organized entries. Then he came across a series of pages she'd scribbled all over. He had about half the papers picked up and loosely held in one hand when two words written in bold caught his attention.

His name had been centered at the top of a page filled with chicken scratch. Much of the original information had been marked out, the edges and back of the page rewritten in haphazard order. It was nothing like the organized content of the original page, but rather a haphazard compilation of notes—very, very personal notes.

She'd documented their time together in a weird shorthand that made no sense, beginning with "storm sex on way to ranch" to "voice of a professional country artist" and ending with "confrontation with brother, revelations of physical abuse as a child, broken relationship, wounded—so wounded. See journal."

His hand involuntarily fisted, crumpling the single sheet of paper. *Journal? She'd written about his private, not-for-business-consumption life in some journal?*

His gut plummeted and he lost his balance, the papers he'd held in his opposite hand falling away without notice or care. They sifted to the floor, some settling over his boots, others hitting the polished hardwood floor and sliding to a stop several feet away.

She'd heard at least part of the fight with Eli and hadn't said a word, hadn't told him.

Cade had counted on the music in the cabin to mute their voices. He'd been a fool.

Whipping around, he stared at the window anew. It had to have been open. But why wouldn't she have announced herself? Why listen in on a conversation that obviously didn't involve her? She hadn't struck him as that type of woman.

He rounded on the table, realization dawning slow and dull like the sunrise on a stormy day. She'd come to him *after* making her notes, notes that identified him as abused, broken, wounded. Had he been nothing more than a pity fuck? Had she come to him to heal him in her own way?

He pulled his hat off and shook his head, trying to clear it. No. She'd said she loved him. She hadn't said that out of pity. *Had she?* No. No, no, no. What they'd shared hadn't been about pity. She hadn't known anything about him when they came together in the storm. That joining—it had been sudden.

His gaze shifted to the fallen paperwork. He began gathering it rapidly, scanning page after printed page of notes. She'd researched each guest for the inaugural thoroughly, leaving an occasional note in the margins. That was acceptable.

What *wasn't* acceptable was that it was clear she'd gone on to document upcoming events with these people, opportunities for her to recover lost ground in the PR and marketing fields. She'd made notes on means and methods of discussing these opportunities with each individual while he or she was at the ranch and at her disposal, and had even assigned names—*her staff members?*—to follow up and ensure her company had the opportunity to bid on future projects.

With the exception of a couple of travel magazines, very few of Emma's notes documented how Lassos & Latigos Dude Ranch was going to benefit.

He shoved the loose papers he'd collected into the blue binder and opened the green one. Inside were pages filled with notes on amending the guest list, last-minute changes involving names he didn't recognize, a frequent flyer program number, notes on tickets purchased last night and more. But there was nothing noted on the pages regarding what these names meant for the ranch, what the individuals might do for Lassos & Latigos or how the Covingtons might recognize a long-term return-on-investment for the money they'd paid her to organize this event.

Moving with extreme care, he picked up both binders and made sure he fed the three-hole-punched pages onto the rings. He didn't want to lose a single sheet.

Eli needed to see this. He'd know what to do. He'd be able to look at it and assure Cade it was all a huge misunderstanding. And if Eli couldn't, Emma could. She *would*. Because no way had she done what it seemed she'd done.

No way had she sold out the ranch for her own benefit.

No way had she planned to use him…and then told him she loved him.

13

EMMA COULDN'T BREATHE. There was likely a handful of viable reasons—nerves, Cade, pending panic attack, Cade, anxiety, Cade, nerves again—but none of those were wholly responsible. No, the fundamental reason she couldn't draw a deep breath were the jeans Reagan had finally deemed "perfect."

They fit Emma like a second skin, or even a first skin if you were counting the fact the pockets actually seemed riveted to her butt. She'd have a permanent *W* from the Wrangler logo branded on her backside before long—if it wasn't already there. She was too scared to take the jeans off to check. Taking them off would mean she'd have to stuff herself back into them, and Reagan had left her here at the cabin less than twenty minutes ago, saying she didn't want to be here when Cade showed up.

Cade.

Just the thought of him made the butterflies attempt to flutter against the front panel of her jeans. She hadn't seen Cade all day. Probably best, since she couldn't believe she was doing this, going out with him like this after professing to love him. It was so backward. Simple *dating* didn't happen for her at home. Who had time? But here, in the remote hills and in the shadows of the wild New Mexico mountains? Apparently she was a different woman. And if she was, it was all because of him.

Walking across the room, she laughed as she tried to swing her hips. Under no delusion did she appear sexy. Instead, she assumed she looked far more like someone with severe back problems trying to make her way across a room while in debilitating pain. Poor Cade. He'd have to lay her out across the bench seat of the pickup and then pull her out at the restaurant. She'd be the cowgirl version of the kid in the snowsuit in *A Christmas Story*. They'd have to eat leaning against the bar because there would be no sitting down. And if she got her sock twisted in her boot? She was so screwed because she doubted she could bend over. Of course, her ass looked *amazing*, but that was inevitable in jeans this "fitted," as Reagan had called them.

Emma laughed and ended up gasping for breath. *Was it worth it just to ensure her ass was the best on the dance floor?* Glancing in the mirror that hung by the front door, she did a little shimmy. Vanity might be the death of her, but damn if she wasn't hot when they buried her.

Then there was the top. Emma tugged at the hem, more than a little self-conscious. The sleeveless white shirt was stark and crisp against the dark blue denim and black boots. The shirt wasn't long enough to meet the waistband of the jeans, but exposed roughly two inches of skin all the way around, tying in the front beneath all of three silver Concho buttons.

She'd explained to Reagan she was nervous that Cade would consider her inappropriately dressed. It seemed odd to put so much effort into her appearance with plans to have fun over dinner and dancing, and then work to create enough distance between them there would be no accusations of impropriety when the other guests arrived. She was sure he wouldn't be keen on her plan, but a client affair was the last thing her firm could afford to have publicized, particularly when it involved the owner.

Emma wandered to the window and pulled the curtain aside, attempting to be casual as she tried to see if Cade was near. That's when it struck her. There was nothing going on out there but a good, stiff breeze strong enough to make the evergreens planted beside her cabin lift and fall back with each gust. Yet nothing blew over her skin beyond the cabin's air-conditioning.

Her window, the same one she'd opened last night, was closed and locked.

Someone had been in here...with all the paperwork scattered.

He'd left at daybreak and would have walked right past the window. For the space of a heartbeat, her entire system shut down. Cade would have come in to close the window, the *screenless* window, left open to the elements.

"No." The single word was more plea than declaration as every system came back online with a rush of fear-fueled adrenaline. If he'd shut the window and left, great. But if he'd looked at the paperwork...

She spun so quickly she nearly tripped in her rush to reach the little workstation. She breathed easy. Both her folders were there. If he'd been inside the cabin to fix her window, he'd have seen the binders and...

The papers. The papers are all wrong.

She'd left them scattered across the little table after making call after call. And the phone. It had been returned to the little pass-through into the kitchenette.

Her fingers were numb as she flipped the blue binder

open. The papers she'd left scattered all over were now organized and in alphabetical order.

He'd read them. Read all her notes on how she could both establish the dude ranch and save her company. But without context, without explanation, she understood exactly how he'd have interpreted the documentation.

Hands trembling violently, she slowly opened the green notebook. The pages were organized. That hardly registered. Her focus was locked on an envelope that had been placed inside. An envelope with the ranch's logo and mailing address on the upper left corner, and her name—Ms. Emmaline Graystone, President— followed by her Manhattan office address formally printed in rough, handwritten script on the front.

And she knew. Eli would have printed the address off the computer. Ty, being the youngest and most likely to defer to his oldest brother, would have probably left the task for Eli. But Cade—Cade would have made this as personal for her as it was for him.

Her hands shook so hard she ended up ripping the envelope open, decimating the paper. Inside was a check in the amount due her firm for services rendered sans optional performance bonus per their contractual agreement.

She dropped the check and looked for a note. *Nothing.* Driven by an emotional panic she couldn't name, she shook the binders, pages down, dug through the small pockets front and back and did a cursory flip through the pages.

She found nothing because he'd left nothing. Just the check. A cold, final closing of the door on what might have been.

She shouldn't have expected otherwise. Not really. The Covingtons wouldn't engage in a major confronta-

tion; there would be no screamed allegations or asser-
tions of wrongdoing. That wasn't the Covington way.
They might deal with each other in such a straightfor-
ward manner, but never, ever did they deal so directly
or take such a hard line with those outside their intimate
fold. And this? This said she'd been officially evicted.

She traced the sharp edge of the linen envelope. The
smart thing to do would be to go to the house and face
the music. But she couldn't. She didn't have it in her to
leave here with the recriminations and hateful words
Cade would hurl at her, no matter that he probably had
some right. Instead, she would, for once, allow herself
to be a coward. She'd return to Manhattan, to her apartment and to a life where she had no friends close enough
to commiserate with. There'd be no one to share the
truth—that she'd fallen in love with a cowboy—no one
to hold her as she explained she'd ultimately failed to
survive the fall.

Shivers rocked her. What she wouldn't do to go back
and make this right. She'd been in over her head when
she'd taken the ranch job from Michael. After all, what in
the name of the heavens did a city girl know about marketing a dude ranch? Nothing—that's why she'd handed
over the bulk of the work to him in the first place.

Desperate for the business, she'd trusted him to do his
job as she did hers. She'd been assured repeatedly that he
had the Covington contract under control. She'd been so
busy trying to shore up her other accounts, she'd had to
trust him to forge new contacts and open new avenues
they could pursue in the future.

Instead, he'd been taking money from the company
and then set her up to fail with the Covington account.
Only she'd ruined herself much more thoroughly than
he could ever have imagined.

From the beginning, she'd let others take control of her life. First her parents, then Michael and, most recently, Cade. That ended here. She'd salvage the only thing she could now—her business.

Eyes stinging, she unbuttoned the jeans and tried not to laugh as the zipper voluntarily slid down with almost inanimate relief. Catching the heel of her boots in the horseshoe bootjack, she pulled them free one at a time and then pulled off the jeans. She tucked the boots under the edge of the sofa, and then folded the jeans along the sharp, starched crease. She took her top off and folded it, too, placing it on top of the jeans. Moving blindly to the bedroom and her suitcase, she pulled out a pair of linen pants, a tank and a matching white linen blazer. She couldn't bring herself to care about the wrinkles. Standard nude platform heels to give her a little height and she was dressed.

She'd have to call a car service to pick her up and deliver her to the Amarillo airport. It would take the service forever to arrive, but she now had nothing on her hands but time. Depression pulled at her, an ugly darkness that encouraged her to lie down and give in. It would be so easy, to give in and sleep until she could flee, but all the same emotions would still be here when she woke.

The knowledge didn't stop her from flopping onto the bed and staring at the waxed, tongue-and-groove pine ceiling. The ceiling fan circled fast enough to create eddies of cool air but not fast enough to dry the tears rolling down her temples.

"I wasn't meant for this, was never meant to be loved. I wasn't raised with that genetic predisposition to give my heart away. Damn you. Damn you, Cade Covington," she whispered to the empty room.

She'd been so cautious, so careful about their emotions, but what had been an unplanned fling had taken on a life of its own. It revolved around him, around her winning his hard-earned laughter, digging out more frequent smiles, touching him deeply—and then destroying everything with notes that made it clear she'd had ulterior motives for the job. It was all the proof he'd ever need to validate his original belief that Emma didn't fit—not on the ranch, not in the community, not in the lifestyle and, above all, not in his life. Worse, she was terrified it would be the last nail in the emotional coffin where he'd buried his belief in himself as a man of worth. For that, she'd never forgive herself.

She stood, intent on going to him at the same time as a sharp knock sounded. The reverberation had her racing, half-blinded by tears, for the front door. She yanked it open, his name already on her lips.

"No, ma'am. I'm sorry. My name is Alex. I'm with Sagebrush Limousine service. I was contracted to take you to the airport."

She fought to keep her knees from buckling. The check hadn't been Cade's official goodbye.

This was.

CADE VIBRATED WITH unchecked fury as he watched the shuttle driver load Emma's bags into the large SUV. Emma hadn't mustered the nerve to come up here and defend herself.

After reading the notes and making a couple of calls to incoming guests, Eli had come to the same conclusion Cade had. The guests had confirmed that Emma's firm had solicited them for this event. And that the firm was bidding on upcoming events for each respective company. But the bids didn't involve the ranch. Nor did they involve Emma. Cade had insisted Eli ask. The clients had been working with her vice president, Michael Anderson. The man had done the follow-up work on the Covington contract. All of it.

Cade had maintained it was possible Emma didn't realize what had been done in her absence.

Eli had only scoffed. "This is corporate America, brother. She knew what she was doing long before she got on the plane at LaGuardia."

"You left her a note, Cade. You told her we wanted her explanation, more specifically that *you* wanted her explanation, about what her notes meant." Reagan glared at Eli. "You're cynical, Eli. That doesn't mean you have to be a bastard to the woman your brother loves."

Eli went still even as Cade erupted off the couch. "I don't love her!"

"Settle down, bro," Ty said from his reclined position near the hearth, eyes closed and his fingers laced together over his lower abdomen. He crossed one foot over the other and cracked his eyelids so only slits of his dark brown irises were visible. "You're a lot of things, but you're not a liar. Ever. Not even to…" He trailed off and he let his head loll to the side so he could look out the front window toward the single lit guest cabin. "No, *especially* not to yourself. You've always taken the full brunt of the truth." He sat up and leaned his forearms on his knees as he faced Cade. "I never thanked you."

Cade's heart stopped beating. It must have, because he suddenly couldn't breathe, couldn't hear over the rushing noise in his ears, couldn't see past the black spots that dotted his vision. He managed to croak out a single word. "What?" Feminine hands guided him to sit, but he gently slipped free of their grasp. "What did you just say, Tyson?"

His younger brother's head dipped low. "You heard me."

Cade rounded on his eldest brother. "You want to explain?"

Eli glanced at Reagan. She gave a short nod and left the room. Eli looked at Cade, his face traced with the unbearable weight of a burdened conscience. "I didn't break your trust. He heard us last night, Caden."

"Half the place heard you last night," Ty muttered.

"Not helping," Eli said to his younger brother softly before rising to face Cade. "Ty came to me, demanded answers." The older man rolled his shoulders and looked away before speaking. "I can't lie to him, Cade. Not even to salvage your misguided sense of honor."

"Misguided?" Cade bit out. "You should have come to *me*, Tyson. I'm the one you heard spill his guts." Cade's chest ached so bad he thought his heart was failing him. "Why? Why go to Eli when he was never here?" He rubbed the heel of his hand over his heart hard enough to ball up his shirt and chafe skin.

"Hell, Cade. I didn't—*don't*—know *how* to go to you with this stuff." Ty's soft admission seemed painful.

Cade stepped forward and wrapped his little brother in his arms, holding him as they both shook with the effort to divert the tears. In the end, it was pointless. Emotion overwhelmed the three brothers when Eli's large hands lay gently on each man's shoulder. Wounds long scarred over were opened, memories Cade had buried were resurrected, branded and burned by the love these two men, his two brothers, had for him.

He watched out the picture window as the hired SUV drove away and carried in it the one chance he might have had at setting the rest of his life straight. Had she come to him, he would have found a way. Even in the midst of this unexpected heartbreak and renewal, he would have chosen her. All he'd asked in the letter he'd left for her was that she allow love to be enough, that she make the choice to put him in front of her career.

But she hadn't.

14

THE CHECK EMMA had left lying on the cabin floor was mailed to her three times. She returned it four. It was then that the brothers, or Reagan as the bookkeeper, must have realized she'd never accept it and stopped resending it. Part of her longed to find it in her mailbox simply as a means of connection to the memories. That part was small. The majority of her was reduced to one giant, exposed nerve every time she saw the ranch's logo. It wasn't enough of him. It was too much.

She'd planned to fire Michael Anderson as soon as she got the evidence against him she needed. Instead, the clever bastard handed her sales figures proving he'd created viable contacts through the ranch's inaugural event—which had been a huge success even though no representative from her firm had been there—and through Michael's other accounts. Through the summer months that followed, the firm's revenues climbed more than 58 percent. He assumed that secured his position, but Emma was in control now. She knew what he'd attempted to do to her with the ranch contract. All she had to do now was wait for the right moment.

In the meantime, she'd refunded to the Covingtons

every dime they'd paid plus 7 percent interest. They deserved to make *something* for what they'd been put through. Quietly, she also directed traffic to their website and their bookings page, and had continued to anonymously send brochures to premier travel agencies around the world as she learned more and more about how the ranch account should have been handled in the first place.

As the last of summer folded away and the mornings became crisp, she was walking to work, her mind wandering where it always did when undisciplined—straight to Cade Covington. She couldn't help but wonder what the change of seasons would be like in northern New Mexico versus Manhattan. Here, the pungent smell of hot asphalt and the craze of summer tourism had finally begun to die down. The air seemed cleaner, and the last of the afternoon heat quickly faded to the first chilly reminders that winter was next and would have her due. There? No doubt the trees would change, the aspens burning yellow in the setting sun, the cottonwoods would turn a rich orange, the hardwoods would be a medley of colors interspersed by both tall and shrubby evergreen cedars. The grass would soften to a buttery yellow before going dormant long before the first hard freeze. Tourism would peak and then die until the first snowfall. Not that she'd checked, looked up pictures or kept an eye on their weather, or anything.

How would the ranch do over the winter? Would the Covingtons benefit from her hard push for holiday family gatherings in the scenic Southwest? Or would they choose to close the ranch for Christmas and have a family holiday of their own? So many questions she'd never have the answers to, never be part of.

Then there was the upcoming wedding. Reagan's last

name would officially become Covington on the second Saturday of October. It was impossible not to envy the woman. Beyond the constant regret she lived with regarding Cade, Emma was most sorry to miss the wedding.

She slipped out of the main foot traffic thoroughfare and leaned against the closed iron-grated windows of an electronics shop. Her lungs worked like bellows, her breath condensing on the crisp air. She closed her eyes at the sting of tears.

She'd wanted everything she'd experienced at the Covington ranch—a successful business, a house that was a home and family inside those four walls. *Family.* She had no idea how to make it happen. Sure, she could get pregnant, but that wasn't the type of family unit she wanted, craved, needed. Those three factors, down to the last emotional kernel each word held, had roused her dreams of having a family of her own one day.

She'd wasted enough time waiting to be sure of her next step, had spent far too long worried about being wrong again. She had to reclaim her life and put her goals in motion once more and assume responsibility for every aspect of life. Starting now.

Emma rejoined the heavy foot traffic and rounded the corner to her office building, absently greeting the doorman. Filing into the next available elevator, she called out, "Fourteen," when someone near the button panel asked for floors.

The elevator started its way up, depositing her on the fourteenth floor. Her company held one half of this floor. There were three additional floors above her, and while she'd busted her butt to get where she was today, yet it had always hovered near the back of her mind that she wouldn't be content until her company worked out of the top floor.

After this morning's revelation, the whole idea seemed wasteful. Life was more than which floor a person occupied, what her bank ledger showed, how profitable her company was on Dunn & Bradstreet, and more. This was just one more thing that would change—this insane pursuit of perfection. She didn't know what she'd expected would happen if she ever attained it. Maybe her parents would contact her from the great beyond to share their approval and pride?

"Not likely, Graystone," she murmured, walking down the hall.

Footfalls silent on the plush carpet, she entered Suite 1410. Immediately the sound of her footsteps changed, her heels now clicking across the marble-tiled lobby, past reception with a friendly good morning and down the hardwood halls to her corner office.

"Hey, Sabra," Emma said, holding out the extra coffee she'd carried in for her personal assistant.

"You brought me a caramel soy mocha latte. Therefore, I am your willing minion on this crisp Monday morn," the woman intoned, eyes closed in bliss.

Emma laughed. "We should do a little career planning. I've left you behind this desk too long."

Sabra's eyes flashed wide. "What? Oh. Oh! That would be great. I'm available at your convenience. Just say when."

It felt good to leave the other woman grinning. What followed wasn't going to be nearly as pleasant. "Do me a favor and ask Michael to come down, would you? I want to talk to him before the day gets any older." Sabra opened her mouth to comment, but Emma gave a single shake of her head. "I don't want you to get involved in what might turn ugly. Please make the call and tell him I want him in my office in the next five minutes."

The raw emotion of Emma's request made Sabra move quickly and quietly to her workstation.

With heavily moderated movements, Emma crossed her office and stared out the nearest floor-to-ceiling window. Below her, sidewalks teamed with people, the street was full of black and yellows and street vendors hawked coffee and pastries to those who'd missed breakfast. The city was so alive, and she pulled on its energy as she mentally composed the very things she'd put off saying for months.

A sharp knock preceded the opening of her office door before she had a chance to offer an invitation to enter. Michael Anderson strode in, his face passive, his eyes not. "Before you say anything, you should know that I'm well aware you've been working on what's supposed to be a closed account."

"I'm going to assume you're referring to the Covington account, though I'm not sure why you've taken such a personal interest in how I handled it." Emma slipped into her chair and crossed her legs, casually resting her elbows on her armrests and steepling her fingers in front of her.

"I had my doubts about giving you that account in the first place, and my doubts were confirmed. After your frankly unethical behavior at the ranch, my legwork was the only thing that saved the firm extreme embarrassment."

Did he know what had happened between her and Cade? Had he followed up with the Covingtons under the pretense of ensuring their satisfaction and found out what had really happened? It was the only way any of them might have spoken about her involvement with

Cade. The thought didn't sit right with her, though. The Covingtons kept their family issues to themselves and, for a very short time, Cade had made her part of that group. No, there had to be a different reason he'd claimed she'd behaved inappropriately. Maybe one of the cowboys had talked? But their loyalty ran deep, too. Perhaps a contractor? In the end, it didn't matter. She had a card up her sleeve, too.

"I had my doubts about you, too. So I asked our accountant to pay special attention to your reports over the last few months."

He shut the door with more force than necessary before storming forward, planting his fists on her desk and looming over her.

Before he could speak, she leaned her chair back and let a small, indifferent smile play over her face. "Power moves don't impress me, Michael. They never have. Take a seat or get out," she said with soft assurance.

He slowed his breathing and pushed off her desk. He stood and straightened his jacket and tie before gracefully sinking into one of the chairs opposite her. "I'm sure he found my work to be without reproach. *Your* behavior, on the other hand, was a direct contradiction to the hard line you and I agreed we'd take regarding personal involvement with clients. I'm your vice president, Emma, and you owe me an explanation."

"And just what, exactly, do you believe you know about my behavior?" she asked, her tone far less moderated, far more lethal than she'd intended. When he didn't respond, Emma focused on her fingertips, fighting to keep them pressed together to disguise the fact her hands shook. "Given the fact you've worked for me for seven years, I'm quite shocked you have nothing to say.

Or maybe it's just easier to foster gossip behind my back before you actually try to take me out with it."

Michael stared at her, his face cold, fine lines showing at both the corners of his thinned lips and narrowed eyes.

She might have bought the cold shoulder of offense if sweat wasn't already beading at his hairline, or if the foot he'd crossed over his knee hadn't begun to vibrate rapidly, rhythmically. Those two things revealed everything she needed to know. "Your tells give you away." Dropping her hands, she pushed to stand and walked around her desk. Closing in on him, she rested one hip on the corner and let a leg dangle, her hands gripping the desk's edge. "Go on, say it to my face."

He tugged at his shirtsleeves and stood, moving to put the chair between them so he was farther out of her reach. "When I was reviewing your binders, I found the letter. The one that outlines your failure to operate in good faith."

A letter. The impact of that simple statement rocked her so hard she couldn't catch her breath. Fighting to remain completely neutral, she vowed to herself to get that letter back. First? She was going to deal with this SOB.

Leaning toward him, her bared teeth were more threat than smile. "You're going to produce that letter immediately, or I'll be filing a professional complaint with the Global Alliance for Public Relations and Communications Management before lunch."

"You can't file against your own employee," he sputtered. "You'll implicate the firm."

Despite her frantic desperation to get her hands on that letter, she watched Michael fight to remain in his seat. She found herself suddenly ashamed to have bought into the corporate mantra that he'd brought with him.

He'd professed loud and long that any business was

better than no business, that a person did what he had to do to secure an account and keep the business growing. But that philosophy had completely undermined her dreams for what the company should have been. She'd wanted a company clients chose because they knew what they'd get when they came to her door: ethics, honesty, skilled marketing and personal service. None of the big business, assign-an-impersonal-team approach, but rather an account manager and two or three team members that the client could contact directly in the event their account manager was out.

The truth hit her broadside. *That's the very same thing Cade wanted for the dude ranch—to keep it personal, not let it become a corporate giant that ate up the foundation of his beliefs.*

It was when he believed she'd understood, when he was certain he'd seen in her that same philosophy that he'd opened up. And she knew with certainty that whatever was in that letter would change everything.

"I've been such a fool," she murmured.

Michael stood, shoulders square, and moved out of her reach.

Emma stood herself and faced him. "I'm not done with you."

Michael snorted. "Right. Well, I have more pressing things to do than listen to your empty threats. You file against me, I'll reveal exactly what happened between you and the middle Covington brother."

Emma's stomach went into free fall. "Pardon me?"

"I know you slept with him. What was his name? Carl?"

"Cade. His name is Cade." And Michael was lying. No one in Manhattan knew anything about what had happened on the ranch. Besides, Cade would never have mentioned their liaison in a letter. *Any* letter. "Like so many things about you, your allegations are false, Michael. I've been home for months, and not a single word has passed through these hallways about my behavior— good, bad or otherwise."

"Not yet," Michael said softly. She leaned against the desk, and considered her next move. That he believed he knew what had passed between Cade and her made her sick, but she wouldn't give him the upper hand in this. Not now, and not ever. It might have been history at this point, but…

Her heart constricted as if someone had tightened an invisible fist around it. No matter that Cade hadn't contacted her. No matter that what had developed between them was clearly done in his mind. Emma still loved Cade. It seemed nothing would change that.

Michael crossed his arms and smiled. "I know for a fact you haven't seen the letter, so you have no idea what's in it."

Her eyes narrowed. "You feel so superior? Enlighten me."

"It was addressed to you but not opened." Michael smiled. "I took the liberty of opening it. Quite touching, really."

She knew she paled, but couldn't help it. "You're going to return those files to me in their entirety, Michael, or I will contact the authorities with what our accountant uncovered." He started to object and she leaned in close enough to tell he'd had some kind of spicy sausage for breakfast. "Are you so sure that you covered your tracks?"

"I can make it seem that you and I were skimming that money off the company's revenue together," he whispered harshly. "And like I said before, you take me down, you're going down with me. You can't file allegations of impropriety against me without implicating yourself as the sole owner of the company. You sign off on all our reporting," he said on a sneer. "Seems your little power play has backfired, Emma."

An acerbic grin spread across her face. "Possibly. But you're operating on the assumption you're an active employee with plausible credibility. What, in all of this, have I said that leads you to believe you're still employed?" She picked up her phone and rang security, asking for an escort out of the building for a potentially hostile former employee. Then she got her assistant on the line and told her to lock Michael's door. If he approached, Sabra was to call 9-1-1.

His eyes widened. "You can't—"

"I just did. You're fired, Michael."

CADE SAT ATOP his horse and gazed out over the herd. The cows they'd kept looked good. Those that had survived the Shipping Fever infection had regained the majority of the body mass they'd lost, and most of them were coming in pregnant. Funny what a year of decent grass, on-site medical care and gentle handling would generate in the way of returns.

Cowboys called to one another and their charges as they moved the herd toward a pasture nearer the house. Each ranch hand was paired with four guests—two males, two females. Guests showed up Saturday morning and stayed to help move cattle around before they left. Then the ranch's cowboys, directed by Reagan, would preg-check the cows that had been brought into the working field by running them through portable pens and chutes. Then, next week's guests would help push the pregnant cows to a nearby pasture and the open—or nonpregnant—cows to a far pasture for ease of management through the coming winter and birthing season.

He grinned. Turned out that having "help" that paid him for the privilege of working the Bar C wasn't such a ridiculous idea after all. Hell would freeze before he admitted his feelings to Eli, but he could admit to himself that the whole thing had worked out far better than he'd expected.

As of the end of August, Lassos & Latigos had already exceeded projected first-year revenues by 17 percent. Net. If they could keep this up, financial security would be within reach. He'd be able to sleep at night, to operate with the knowledge that money was actually available when he went to an ATM, to be sure he could make his annual bank note payment without having to consider selling off sections of the ranch. The whole idea made him light-headed.

But there was one missing facet, the biggest piece of all. *Emma.*

What he wouldn't give to have been able to share this particular success with her, even through a simple email. The ever-familiar, unfailingly present tightness spread through the muscles in his shoulders and neck.

It had been four months, one week and two days since she left, but Cade hadn't even begun to recover. Her choice had carved his heart from his chest. He breathed because his brain was too stupid to stop the autonomous action. He ate because his stomach wouldn't stop bitching at him when neglected. He worked long hours because it kept his mind on the tasks at hand. And he slept, every chance he got he slept, because that's where he could coax his memories out to play privately, where he could see her and avoid the hurt, remember the feel of her skin beneath his hands, recall the taste of her on his lips, sweet and rich. But she'd made her choice, and he had to respect that.

Cade's radio beeped. He wheeled Ziggy around, trotting well away from the activity before cuing the mic. "This is Cade."

"It's Eli. Look, there's something I have to own, and it's…this isn't going to be easy, man," Eli said gruffly. "Will you come up to the main house, soon as you can?"

Cade glanced at his watch and then at the cluster of twentysomethings trying to judge how long it would take for them to move the herd into the next field. "Probably less than two hours to get done here, get to the barn, put Ziggy away and make it to the house. That work?"

"Not really."

Cade gripped the radio receiver hard enough the plastic creaked. "What's happened? Everyone okay?"

"Yeah. We're all good. I just hoped to talk to you before everyone was back."

When translated, Cade knew his brother actually meant, "You're going to rage out and I wanted to give your temper a chance to flare, and then cool down before there were witnesses." Forcing himself to relax his grip on the receiver took the majority of his attention. Still, the mental Rolodex he kept of the wrongs done him flipped from one entry to the next, curiosity assessing each one for the urgency Eli deemed this worth. Then he struck The Card, and everything in him chilled before his marrow went molten and his vision narrowed. "Is this about Emma?"

Eli didn't answer, instead letting the silence between them solidify until it was nearly a tangible, immovable wall between them. Cade's curse rang out low and harsh. "I need to get my group reassigned to another wrangler before I can come in, but rest assured I'll be at the house within the hour."

He handed his group of guests off to his ranch manager, Ross, before pointing Ziggy toward the barn and settling him into a comfortable lope. They crossed fields gone dormant with the season's change, the grass no longer gray-green but more a neutral beige hue that colored the entire landscape as the hardwoods lost their leaves.

Emma had wanted to experience the change of seasons. Just the whisper of her name through his mind started the myriad possibilities rolling—she'd become involved with some international playboy-billionaire-lives-on-a-yacht-in-St. Bart's-prince, that she was engaged, that her firm had taken off, that her firm had tanked, that she'd been diagnosed with some deadly disease—that she was dead. By the time he reached that last possibility, he'd spurred Ziggy on, giving the horse his head.

He went straight to the house, looping the horse's reins around the mirror of an SUV before fumbling with the radio, cuing the mic and advising anyone in earshot at main camp where to retrieve and take care of the animal after their mad dash home.

"What happened?" Cade shouted as he opened the front door. He was well into the living room, chest heaving, before he remembered to let go of the radio's controls. "Eli!" he bellowed.

His brother came around the corner, face pale, hands fisted. "Have a seat."

"Is she dead?" Cade managed to wheeze.

Eli's brow furrowed. "Who?"

"Emma." Her name almost burned Cade's lips.

"Dead…" Eli's brow furrowed. "Hell, no. Far as I know, she's fine."

The fight left Cade in a rush and he collapsed into the nearest chair. "You shaved a good three years off my life, and I'm going to owe Ziggy a six-pack of Coke for hauling ass home like I did." Resting his head against the chair, he pulled off his hat and tossed it on the coffee table.

Reagan walked around the corner with a tray of iced tea.

Ty followed.

Prickly fingers of unease skipped up Cade's spine, one vertebra at a time. The sensation came to rest at the base of his skull, initiating a pounding sequence that made him massage the small indention there. Anything to dissuade the ache that spread from his heart to his mind. Whatever had drawn his family together would be bad—really bad if they felt they needed to manage him as a united front. "Someone say something."

Reagan silently handed him three ibuprofen and his glass. He offered a quiet thank-you before gulping the pain reducer down with a single swallow. He only wished the medication would do something about that persistent ache in his chest where his heart should be.

"You were right," Eli started. "This is about Emma, about something that happened the last couple of days she was here."

"Spill it, Eli," Cade all but snarled.

Ty moved to the end of the sofa and sat on the edge, placing himself between his older brothers.

Reagan sank onto the sofa beside Eli, also placing herself between the two brothers. "Your brother loves you more than anything, but it doesn't stop him from being a completely domineering dumbass at times." She glanced at Eli and nodded slowly. "Tell him."

"It's about the letter you wrote her, the letter pleading

with her to meet us here." Eli took a shaky breath. "I'm pretty sure she never saw it before she left."

Cade right eye twitched as he fought to remain calm. "Why?"

"Because I buried it in the paperwork near the back of the second folder."

Before Eli finished his sentence, Cade was out of the chair and headed toward him. "You had no right!" he bellowed.

Eli came to his feet and the two collided, fists swinging. They plowed into the sofa and tipped it over, following it to the ground.

"She was using you!" Eli shouted right before taking a fist to the jaw.

"You can't be sure of that!" Cade ducked, answering Eli's right hook with his own and connecting solidly with the other man's ribs. "That's why I wrote the letter. To give her a chance."

Cold water showered both men before another fist met skin. Sputtering, they both looked up.

"On your feet," Reagan said quietly. When they didn't move fast enough, she went to the kitchen and returned with another pitcher of water. "On. Your. Feet."

The two men rose, both bruised, bleeding and breathing hard. Destruction ruled the room, the sofa would be water stained, the decorative bowl and matching lamp Reagan had recently put out on the coffee and end table were both shattered, and standing water made the floor a slippery mess. "You two—shut it down," she snapped. "Pull up a seat, opposite sides of the rooms." When they didn't move, she shouted at the top of her lungs. "Now!"

Cade shoved Eli and went to reclaim his seat, forced to set it right side up before dropping into it with a wince. *Damn, but this would leave a mark.*

Eli followed suit, but instead of dropping into his chair, he sank down gingerly, favoring one knee.

Reagan stood between them, pale and shaking with what Cade quickly identified as anger. She shocked him senseless when she rounded on Eli. "Who, exactly, do you think you are, Elijah Covington, to set out making decisions for your brother, for his private life and for the ranch's well-being without consulting those of us with a vested interest?" He immediately opened his mouth and she threw more water at him, leaving him sputtering. "Prove you're educated, for once, and choose your words carefully before you speak."

He glared at her, the muscles in his jaw working. The tension grew thick, then thicker still, when Eli refused to answer her.

Reagan moved in closer to him, setting the water pitcher down. "You and Cade have had your differences. That's no secret. But you can't waltz back into his life and presume you know what's best for him. You owe him the courtesy and respect of treating him like the man he's become."

"I 'owe him' the protection I never gave him growing up," Eli ground out. "Emma wasn't just screwing him—she was going to screw him over."

The crack of Reagan's hand meeting Eli's cheek stunned both Cade and Tyson, who only stared at Reagan, wide-eyed. "She wasn't just Cade's lover, Eli. She was my friend. You ripped her out of my life just as much as you ripped her out of his. You'll show Emma some respect, particularly after all the goodwill she's offered us since she left."

"What goodwill?" Cade asked, jumping into the conversation.

Eli lifted his chin. "She refunded full payment to

us, plus interest, within two weeks of returning to New York." On a heavy sigh, Eli leaned forward and rested his forehead in his hands. "There have also been advertising campaigns we haven't paid for that have run in premier travel magazines. No doubt those ads have helped generate business, as have the gift cards she's been giving to clients who review their experience on one of five sites."

Ty scooted forward in his seat. "How's she getting guest names?"

"She's not. The ads offer the cards to anyone who contacts the magazine and provides a bill of sale and proof of their review." Eli finally glanced up.

"Why did you wait until now to tell me?" Cade meant to lob the question like a grenade. Instead, it fell softly and with no threat whatsoever.

"I got a call from the FBI about Michael Anderson. Seems they're investigating him for skimming the books. When I asked Reagan for our records, she got the whole story from me. She made me call you. But I still believe Emma was using you, Cade. The books proved it. Seemed she had a change of conscience at the end, but she used you to get there." Eli swallowed hard. "I wanted to protect you from being hurt again."

Reagan moved close to Eli, gently touching the red mark her hand had left on his cheek. "I'm sorry for this. It wasn't right. But what you did wasn't right, either. She might have been my first true girlfriend, and I might miss her like crazy, but that's a drop in the bucket compared to what Cade's been through. He loves her, Eli. What would you have done if someone tried to terminate our relationship based on their singular opinion that we didn't suit?"

Eli's face hung slack for a moment before a bevy of emotions raced across it, everything from rage to grief to remorse—a giant fifteen-car pileup of emotion colliding there in the living room. He looked at Cade. "Do you…"

Put up or shut up, man. There won't be another chance.

"Yeah." His voice trembled, and he cleared his throat. "Yeah," he said more firmly. "I do." He stood, staring at the floor and ignoring the blooming ache in his ribs as he laced his fingers behind his head and pulled. "I love her." It took him a second to be able to face Eli. "Living without her has been like living with a terminal illness that kills me a little more with every breath I take. She's the cause, and she's the only cure."

A sudden intensity appeared in his older brother's normally stoic gaze. "We'll fix this." Eli stood and moved to Cade. Gripping him by one shoulder, his other hand cupping the side of Cade's neck, Eli lowered his voice. "I've done wrong by you, Cade. Over and over, I've made the wrong decisions where you were concerned. Not that it makes it any better, but every time—*every decision*—was made out of love. Once I make this right with Emma, I'll ask that you forgive me."

One corner of Cade's mouth kicked up as he fought an unexpected rush of emotion for his brother. "Help me get her back, Eli, and the slate's clean. We have to start over somewhere, or we're going to end up killing each other."

Eli grinned and winced as his split lip pulled and bled freely again. "I'd move heaven and hell to earn that clean slate, brother."

Cade shook his head and wrapped Eli in a fierce embrace. "You want to make this right? Between us?"

"More than anything."

"Bring Emma home."

15

EMMA KICKED OFF her high heels, more than ready to drop from five foot ten to her much more moderate five foot six. Today had been another fourteen-hour day on her feet. She'd been in meeting after meeting with staff members, ignoring the speculative gossip about the vice president.

He'd had his little band of supporters, yes, but in general? The rest of the staff despised him, especially when they found out he'd been responsible for the company's recent hardships. And for what seemed like the hundredth time today, Emma berated herself for letting things get so far out of hand, for failing to pay more attention to what he'd been doing and for violating the very concept she'd founded the company on: people.

Curling her toes into her foyer's Oriental carpet, she sighed. Tonight was going to be a beer and wings night. She'd earned it. Her cell phone sat at the top of her briefcase, so she retrieved it, found her favorite sports bar that delivered and hit Call. The phone only rang six times before the bartender answered. She smiled, recognizing his voice. "Hey, Paulie. It's Emma."

"Like I don't recognize that sultry voice from anywhere." The sound of a baseball game was turned down despite the patrons' vocal protests. "Shaddup!" Paulie called out. "There's a lady on the phone. Now, darlin'. What've you been up to that's kept you out of the bar as we gear up for the play-offs? Mets are going to take the pennant race, and you know that leaves them the favorites for the World Series."

"Big dreams, Paulie. Seattle's going to trump the Mets no matter when or where they meet."

"Sacrilege," Paulie whispered in mock horror.

"Doesn't change the fact I miss your wings."

"Now you're talkin'. What can I get you?" His voice had become muffled, and she could imagine him pinching the receiver between his massive jaw and beefy shoulder, order pad at the ready.

"I need—" her phone beeped with an incoming call "—twenty-five wings, bone in, medium sauce, ranch dressing instead of blue cheese, no veggies, a basket of onion rings and a basket of mozzarella sticks, also with ranch dressing."

Paulie chuckled. "Damn, Emma. You havin' a party you didn't invite me to?"

"Nope. It's Friday night, I'm starving and I intend to use your fine food to keep me from having to leave my apartment all weekend."

"You ain't watching chick flicks and gettin' all mopey, are you?"

Paulie's undisguised horror made her laugh. "No. I figured I'd overload on action movies, maybe watch The Avengers twice for good measure." Her phone beeped again, and this time she checked the caller ID. Hard tremors rocked her body and she dropped the phone. Swooping down to pick it up, she all but shouted, "Just deliver it whenever. I've got cash." Then she began jabbing the button to accept the incoming call, but voice mail caught it first.

Still in the foyer, Emma leaned against the front door and clutched the phone with both hands. Her teeth began to chatter. The strangest sense of disembodiment overwhelmed her when her voice mail chimed. She watched as one hand clutched the phone and the other seemed to move of its own accord, hitting Play and then Speaker.

"Emma?"

Her heart stopped.

"This is Reagan. I really need to talk to you. I'm sorry it's taken so long for me to get in touch, but there was a major... Forget it. Bottom line, I'm—surprisingly—still getting married in three weeks and I'm a freaking wreck. You promised to coordinate my wedding for me, and I'm calling that favor in. It's probably not fair of me, but... Emma, I miss you. I don't want to do this without you. Call me at—"

Before Reagan began reciting the numbers, Emma had cut the message off and begun to dial.

Reagan answered on the second ring. "Emma?"

Throat tight, she nodded and gave a sharp, breathy laugh. "Yeah. It's me." She paused, fighting the burn of tears. She'd longed for contact with these people, and here was the one she'd cared about above all but one other. "Reagan." There was a pleading tone she hated but couldn't hide. "Let me explain—"

"Stop." The command was soft but firm. "You don't have to. I know you didn't do us wrong. After all you've done since you left? There's no doubt in my mind."

"But the men..." She forced herself to steady. "Cade."

"I can't control those idiots," Reagan muttered. "And frankly, it's a miracle I'm still marrying my favorite idiot of them all." The other woman chuffed out a short laugh.

"But I can't do it without you. All this crap started arriving two days ago for the wedding, and I have no idea what to do with it. And then I got a notice that FedEx is delivering fresh flowers four days before the event. Not arrangements, Emma. Just *flowers*."

The building mania in ever-calm Reagan made Emma smile. "I'd planned on decorating your cake and doing your flowers. I'll make arrangements for someone from Amarillo to—"

"No." The single, shrill word made Emma wince. "I don't want 'arrangements,'" Reagan choked out. "I want *you*. You're my only girlfriend. All these men will be here, and as hard as I've tried to get Tyson to wear a dress and be my maid of honor, he's being a jerk and refusing on 'testicular principals,' whatever those are."

"I can't go back there, Reagan." The words killed Emma, ripping at wounds that had healed superficially at best. "I won't risk ruining your day by having a confrontation with any of the men."

"There won't be a single derogatory word, look, glance or innuendo in private conversation. I guarantee it."

That hard-edged delivery was almost enough on its own to make Emma believe her. Almost. "I'll make sure you have everything you need," she began again, but Reagan simply interrupted her once more.

"I need *you*, you stubborn woman. Please. Not only for the cake and flowers and stuff, but I need someone to stand up for me at the altar, someone to represent my side." The woman's voice dropped. "I've got no one to go through this with me, Emma. I want you here. Please."

She'd do anything for this woman who'd become so dear to her in such a short time. But she had to know.

"What does Cade think about me being at the ranch again?"

"He's fine with it."

Emma's silence said everything her racing mind couldn't.

"I swear to you, he'll be nothing but a gentleman and he won't bark, or bite, once. I may suck at the feminine stuff like dresses and decorating and flowers and such, but I'm hell with a scalpel. Everyone will be on his or her best behavior. If you say no, I'm just going to keep calling until you're so exhausted you concede."

The thought of being back on the ranch, back in the Covington fold, even if it was only this one last time, pulled at Emma and made her want nothing more than to say yes. "Promise me I can leave if it gets too uncomfortable for me." Reagan hesitated in her answer, and Emma pressed her. "I want your word, Reagan Matthews. I have to be absolutely sure I have a getaway car in the event things go south."

"I promise," she whispered.

Emma wiped at the sweat trickling down her temple. "When do you want me there?"

"First flight you can catch…and as soon as you find a bridesmaid's dress."

"Color preference?" she asked. "Length? Style? Fabric?"

"Don't care. Anything dark will get dusty, so you make the call there. My gown's ivory."

"I picked it out, Reagan," Emma responded, laughing.

"Right. I'm not nervous or anything."

"I've got this covered. I have to make a few arrangements before I can leave, so expect me Wednesday." Memories of her first visit to the ranch rushed over her.

"I'll rent a car," she almost shouted. "Please don't send anyone to pick me up."

"He'll be good, Emma." There was a quiet conviction there. "I swear."

"I'm not worried about that part." *Not too much, anyway.*

"Then why are you so anxious about seeing him?"

Emma's heart tripped, skipped a beat, and then began hammering like a heavy-metal drummer. "It's…" She rubbed the heel of her hand over her sternum, fighting to breathe. "Some things aren't worth revisiting, Reagan. Heartache's one of them. See you Wednesday."

Call disconnected, Emma sagged against the wall. Uncertainty swam through her. Had she said too much? Not enough? Indicated she was over Cade? Or worse, had she indicated that she wasn't? Because what she'd said to Reagan had been the absolute truth—some things, like heartache, *weren't* worth revisiting. But there was a worse consequence, one she feared far more. That she'd get a reunion with the only man she'd ever loved and realize the most she'd ever have from him were the memories, both those from before he hated her and now these, after. Then he'd close the door on her forever.

She had set her life in order, put her business on track once again and made the changes in the business that would allow her to move forward. Even better the company had quickly become financially solvent with Michael gone. He'd been charged with falsifying financial documents and unsound business practices resulting in intentional financial harm. It had all happened so quickly, she'd spun for two weeks solid.

But now that the spinning had stopped, she knew she still wasn't where she was supposed to be. Her skin felt too tight in Manhattan, her opportunities too small. She was one of more than a thousand advertising firms her size. Her creativity was stifled. In order for clients to truly value her, she had to have the space to be unique. Maybe after the wedding she'd scope out opportunities in the Southwest, set herself up as a very small firm doing the kind of one-on-one work with clients whose companies she could really get behind—small accounts that would reach large markets. Clever advertisements that made a company's name stick. Things she'd dreamed of doing before her parents pushed her to be *more*, always more. She understood now that it wasn't settling to be happy. It was settling if she wasn't.

Yes, Emma would make a clean break after the wedding and seize the chance to open a new chapter in her life. It was terrifying, but if the past few months had taught her anything, it was that memories were cold bed partners.

EMMA COMES BACK to the Bar C today. It was all Cade had been able to think about, counting down the days to her arrival once Reagan had gotten her to agree to return. And today, the moment Emma stepped foot on the ranch, he would experience his emotional ground zero.

He'd been recalcitrant about having someone else pick her up, but Reagan had put her foot down. No one was going to pick Emma up. She wanted the chance to get her bearings, and a rental car would give her an element of safety while she was here.

"Like a rental car's going to save her," he muttered to himself, rinsing his soapy hands and drying them on a dishcloth.

But Reagan, who sat at the little desk off the breakfast nook, heard him, anyway. Tired of the administrative work, she'd insisted they get someone to handle the dude ranch's books so she could focus on her vet practice again. To a man, no one had objected but had, instead, supported her request.

The response he received was accompanied by a withering stare. "You're a smart man, Cade. Try to put yourself in her shoes. Coming out here at all took a heck of a lot of guts on her part. She needs to feel like she can get away from all of us, particularly *you*, if things go badly."

Tyson, who'd been lying prone on the sofa, hat covering his face, chuckled. "That's a funny image—you in her shoes. I personally liked the red stilettos, but her boots were pretty hot, too. You could pull off either, bro. Just work the walk."

Too wound up to take much teasing, Cade reached over and, with the dishtowel he'd been using, popped Ty on his T-shirted stomach. His little brother yelped and fell off the sofa, dragging an authentic laugh from somewhere deep in Cade's chest. Even to him, the sound was rusty. The look on Reagan's face, one of surprised joy, only made him more self-conscious. "What? I laugh."

"Not in months," she said, pulling him down for a quick kiss to the cheek. "And never enough."

Heat suffused his face and he fled for the kitchen, but not before an empty plastic soda bottle bounced off his head.

"Be glad I didn't have something heavier," Ty called.

"Like what?" Cade answered without slowing. "Morals?"

"Hey, you're the one who jumped the guest on the way home from the airport, brother." The smile in Ty's voice rendered the words teasing, not biting. "You set a new bar for me. I leap and I leap, but so far I can't clear that bar."

"Shut up," Cade ground out, heat spreading and deepening across his face until he was now flushed a healthy red.

"Sir, yes, sir," Ty all but shouted. "I'll be out at the barn if she shows up and you can't handle her."

Cade put the dishes away with minimal conversation, doing his best to keep from staring at the office clock and watching the hands snap by. He hated the way the red second arm clicked forward and shuddered enough it seemed to settle back before advancing again. Time couldn't move backward, so it shouldn't appear that it did.

"What're you scowling at?" Eli asked, wandering into the kitchen. He grabbed the orange juice from the fridge and plucked a glass Cade had just washed from the drying rack.

"You do dishes next."

Eli arched a brow. "I'm smart. I use the dishwasher."

"Not this one, you don't." One corner of Cade's mouth lifted up. "Burned up last night. Reagan's researching and ordering a new one now. I'll go into Clayton to pick it up as soon as possible."

"Speaking of the hottest vet in the country," Eli murmured, moving toward Reagan as if she was his homing beacon, his safe harbor, his everything. Reaching her, Cade watched as Eli swept her hair aside and laid a gentle kiss against the side of her neck. "Anything in particular you *want*, my bride? The possibilities are endless."

She tilted her head aside to give him better access. "Sure, now that you're finally awake."

Eli buried his face in her hair and breathed in. "Not my fault you found me irresistible—over and over—last night."

"And, on that note, I'll be vacating the premises to preserve my sense of healthy sexual boundaries." Cade grabbed his hat and sunglasses, then slipped his feet into his boots. "House is yours until we see you open the front curtains."

"You don't have to go, Cade," Reagan called.

"Yes. Yes, he does." Eli's statement elicited a very feminine shriek of delight as Cade started down the hall.

Cade shut the front door behind him gently, fighting the unexpected pang of jealousy. He didn't covet his brother's soon-to-be wife, but he undeniably longed for what the man had found with his woman. Cade wanted the same chance to shower Emma with open PDA, to tell her everything she'd meant to him and how her leaving without a goodbye had carved him up like a jack-o'-lantern. Morbidly, he wondered what the pattern would have shown about him and who he'd become.

He found himself approaching the barn's giant sliding door without having chosen the destination consciously. Since the wedding was Saturday, there were no guests until next Wednesday evening. Cade wasn't sorry, even though he'd come to enjoy the guests overall. There were always difficult ones, impossible ones and women seeking to get him into bed, but really? The majority of them were awesome. They respected his way of life, almost revered it, in a way he'd never have imagined. It fulfilled him, sharing who he was and his heritage for all the right reasons. Sending people home with a better understanding of how the past and present ran parallel here, how this hand-to-mouth life gave people food for their tables was incredibly gratifying.

Down the barn's sawdust alleyway, he heard Tyson laugh and say, "Well, what are *you* wearing, gorgeous?"

Cade snorted and shook his head, continuing into the barn. That kid got more tail than the stud he rode, and that was saying something since Gizzy's baby batter was beginning to draw regional attention for the types of colts he consistently threw—big babies with sound temperaments and unmatchable cutting and roping instincts. Tyson might really make a go of a breeding operation if he could get focused, really work the circuit and get his name out there.

But that was none of his business. It was simply something he focused on to keep his mind off the fact that Emma's plane landed in—he glanced at his watch and his body tightened. *Now. Emma's on the ground now.* She'd probably even made it to the rental car kiosk.

His Emma, within reach. He'd never thought to see this day again.

"You okay, Cade?"

He jerked his chin up, blue eyes locking with Tyson's brown ones. "I'm good. Who were you talking to?"

"Roxie here." Ty rubbed the mare's jaw and her longlashed eyes fluttered in bliss. "She's pregnant enough that her regular evening blanket doesn't fit comfortably anymore. Who'd you think I was talking to?"

"No idea. I was half scared to come into the barn on the off chance you had a woman in here." Cade grinned. "You're a player, dude. A *huge* player. Ever think you'll settle down?"

Ty considered the question. "I'll tell you what. I'll settle down when I find a blonde-haired woman who knows as much about genetics and breeding as I do, can put up or shut up in the saddle, is competitive enough to pout every time I beat her in the ring and comes with a dowry large enough to fund a breeding barn. Oh, and Gizzy has to love her madly enough to throw me over for her." He grinned. "Then? You're dang right. I'd snap that woman up in a heartbeat and beg her to take my last name."

Cade's lips twitched. "I've mentally cataloged those

qualities. You're going to end up married if you're not really careful."

Brows winging up, Tyson laughed. "Says the man whose woman is driving in via rental car because Reagan was afraid you'd molest her before you were off airport property."

Cade's mood took a nosedive. "Shut that door before you step all the way through and find I'm just the man to show you you're gettin' a little too big for them britches."

Tyson shrugged. "Beat on me if you want to. It'll just get me more sympathy." His face brightened. "Maybe I can get Mary Ann Calwell to play nurse!"

Cade couldn't help but laugh. "I'm taking Ziggy out to check the fences in pasture fourteen. I'll be in by sundown."

"Avoiding Emma?" The quiet question, devoid of Ty's signature smart-ass humor, caught Cade off guard. "I'm serious, Cade. Are you avoiding her?"

"No." The immediate, honest answer seemed to surprise them both. "I just wanted to get out to ride fence without a gaggle of goslings paddling along behind me." He closed his eyes. "I also need a few minutes to myself, just to get my head straight before she gets here. I have no idea what to say to her. Not right off, anyway. But there's plenty that needs to be said." Cade looked up. "I just have to find my way into the conversation without spooking her."

"Fair enough. Got a radio?"

"I'm responsible enough to know to keep one on me at all times out there." Waving Ty off, he moved to Ziggy's stall and was thrilled to find the gelding alert, listening for his voice. "Ready for a little light work this morning?"

The horse nickered in response, almost as if he'd understood, tossing his head until Cade had to slow the horse down before he got dangerously wound up and too hard to handle. Clipping a lead on Ziggy's halter, he took the horse down to the hitching bar just around the corner from the tack room.

"I've got to get in the saddle and get a little crazy worn off. You up for it, my man?" Cade asked as he cleaned Ziggy's hooves, brushed him down and then saddled up the horse.

As he swung up onto the horse's back, stress from the "Emma Revelation" bled away and Cade took a series of deep, deep breaths. He and Ziggy trotted out of the main pen, breaking into a lope as he hit the first field. Whatever happened, it was going to be all right. He and Emma were going to work this out. No other option was, well, an option.

Operation "Graystone Recovery" was about to get underway.

16

EMMA PULLED THE shiny new 4x4 Chevy Silverado into the semicircular drive and slipped it into Park. The engine ticked like an emotional grenade as it cooled, and Emma couldn't help but wonder at the Fates and their omens.

She hopped down from the truck. The moment her feet hit the dirt, her connection to the place and its people seated itself in her soul. It was a fundamental sense of *knowing*. This was her place. This was where she belonged—home, be it as an employee or as something far greater. She had to fight to keep herself from going there, wishing there had been more for her here than a few days.

The screen door to the house slammed shut and Reagan was on Emma in seconds. "Man, I have missed you." She held Emma at arm's length, critically assessing her appearance. "You seem too thin. You haven't been on some starvation-from-stress diet, have you? I mean it. You're a little underweight. Your boobs were bigger, weren't they?"

Emma laughed as the woman continued to pepper her with questions. Instead of answering, Emma wrapped the taller woman in her arms the best she could. The woman vibrated with a type of energy that both thrilled and crushed Emma. "He's here, isn't he?" she asked quietly. "In the house. Waiting."

"No. He rode out this morning to check fence. Haven't seen him all day." Reagan's brows furrowed. "Given his general response to your return, I'm a little surprised."

Emma swallowed the baseball-sized lump of regret. "It's okay. I really didn't expect him to be here waiting to carry my bags in."

Reagan's face lit but she didn't say anything, just grabbed Emma's hands and held on tight.

"I don't know why not," the deep voice she'd only been able to pull from her memories for more than four months answered. "I'm sort of a gentleman. If I'm fond of you, that is." He paused and she heard the scratch of work-toughened hands on an early five-o'clock shadow. "That or if you're a paying guest. You paying, Emma?"

"No."

"Guess I must be fond of you then. Unlock the truck?"

She fumbled the key fob and it hit the dirt with a muffled clank.

Cade scooped it up before she could respond. "What's with the truck as a rental? I figured you'd be more economically and environmentally conscious."

He was teasing her? Her brows drew together. "I seem to recall someone telling me I'd never get the hang of driving a big-boy truck, so I traded in my Prius and bought a half-ton 4x4 Duramax with the heavy duty Allison transmission." With measured steps, she faced him. "As it happens, I'm a natural, particularly in the city. But that thing was made for dirt roads, not driveways. So I got the same kind of truck from the rental place."

The breeze carried his voice. "What color is your truck?"

"Doesn't matter," she muttered, turning back to Reagan, who watched them curiously.

"I bet the exterior is black or a dark charcoal. Where's the red, Emma?"

Heat crawled up her neck. She'd never survive this visit if he constantly brought up the little things he knew, the little parts of her that he'd tossed away.

"Where?" he demanded.

"I had custom seats installed," she ground out. "Black with red piping."

He responded so softly she almost missed it. Almost, but not quite. "That's my girl."

Grief ripped through her, and it took Reagan grasping her hands to keep her from breaking and running.

"I'll drop your bags in the house, same room." He headed for the main house, his stride long and confident.

"Cabin!" she called after him.

"Nope," he answered casually. "Cabins are for paying guests."

Eyes wild, she found Reagan's gaze zeroed in on her. "I can't. I can't do this, Reagan. I can't sleep with him... I mean next to him. Of course that's what I meant. I can't sleep in the room next to him." She groaned and tipped her face toward the endless blue sky. "I *can't* share a bathroom with him. Proximity clouds my judgment where he's concerned, and I don't want to open wounds that have only just started to heal. Don't make me do this."

"If it were just me, I would put you in any cabin you wanted, but the brothers talked and decided it would be best to have you stay with us."

"Why?" The question lashed out, sharp as the crack

of a bullwhip. "To make sure I don't do anything nefari-
ous in the few days I'm here?"

Reagan started. "You're only staying a few days?"

"I sent you my itinerary." Emma retrieved her hands
and scrubbed them through her hair. "Why?"

"Just hoped you'd be staying longer," Reagan answered on a shrug. "C'mon. Let's get you settled."

"Didn't you hear me?" Emma bit out. "I can't do this."

Reagan paused but didn't face her when she asked,
"Can't or won't, Emma? Because there's a huge difference."

And even though she'd vowed to never misrepresent
anything to the Covingtons ever again, she still struggled before offering the truth. "Won't."

"*Can't* is far less powerful than *won't*, so you'll stay
with us." She resumed her trek to the house, forcing
Emma to either catch up or stand there looking like an
idiot. Seeing as she'd suffered her preset quota of in-
dignities on her initial meeting with Cade, she hustled
to catch up.

THE NEXT FEW days were spent in mad preparation for the
wedding. Reagan tried on her dress to ensure it still fit
fine, flowers were delivered and prepped to hold until
two days before the wedding and the cake came in.
Emma would be sending her favorite local baker a *huge*
tip because he'd managed to figure out how to ship the
layers pre-wrapped in fondant that hadn't shifted, torn,
melted or discolored. It was a miracle. As the cake de-
frosted, Emma made flowers and leaves from fondant
and royal icing, saving a place on each columned layer
for the live floral centerpiece that would decorate it.

Through it all, Cade was right there to help her. Didn't
matter what she asked him to do, he did it without com-

plaint and, more often than not, with some sort of flirtatious suggestion. He frazzled her at first, and she'd had to give herself a stern talking-to the second time she ruined a rose she was spinning out because he'd leaned down and commented about her talent with her hands—a talent he said he'd longed for over the past few months.

Once, he caught her licking the mixer paddle. His eyes had warmed as his lids partially slid down. "I miss that more than your hands." Then he'd gone on about his business. It had distracted her so much that batter dripped down her arm and sleeve. She hadn't cared, the same memories he'd drawn on bombarding her senses and all she could smell was the heat of his skin.

Eli and Ty had been particularly solicitous, making sure she had everything she needed, taking on the job as her cleanup crew when she could shoo Cade out of the kitchen. The help was appreciated, but it meant more people to manage. Apparently, she wasn't the only one with an affinity for cookie dough.

The night before the wedding, Emma nearly fell asleep at the dinner table. Cade, who'd insisted on sitting next to her, pulled her into the warmth of his body. Turning to him, she lost herself in the security of his arms, the smell of sunshine on his flannel shirt, the feel of his hands on her skin and the warmth of his breath in her hair. He shifted her around until he could scoop her up, the change of position waking her.

Groggy, she looked around. "What's going on?"

"Past your bedtime," he'd answered, carrying her to her bedroom downstairs.

"I can get there on my own." Her insistence had been thoroughly interrupted by a jaw-cracking yawn.

"Yeah? I'd argue your GPS has dropped into sleep mode. You'd probably have ended up in the barn."

"I've never slept in a barn," she said into his shirt, fisting the material in one hand as she buried her face in his neck.

"I beg to differ." His husky voice rolled through her, settling deep and low in her belly.

Memories of him taking her against the tack room door had her sighing. "That wasn't sleeping."

"In that case, would you like to sleep with me tonight, Ms. Graystone?"

She sat up so quickly he dropped her—right onto his bed. Emma huffed out a breath. "Really? You're resorting to caveman techniques to get me in here?"

"Not really. You curled into my arms like you belonged there, darlin'. I'm just going with the flow." He sank over her, his lips lowering to hers in a kiss so tender her toes curled. Their tongues touched, soft at first, until need overrode common sense and the familiar passion ignited between them. They fought to breathe each other in, tasting and taking as much as they gave. Hands roamed. Clothing was untucked and skin bared to one another's demanding touch.

Cade groaned into Emma's mouth at the same time her hips lifted involuntarily. He parted her legs and rubbed the hard ridge of his erection against her, the pressure just right to have her mewling her approval.

That sound jerked her out of the moment and she pushed at Cade's chest. "I am *not* sleeping with you. Respect me on this." The ache in her words was so harsh it could have been translated for hearing-impaired onlookers.

"Shame, that." He opened the Jack-and-Jill bathroom door in his room and went inside. Water ran and she heard him brushing his teeth. "If history held true, you would have enjoyed it," he said around his toothbrush, his spirits seemingly jovial.

"You're such a…a…*man*."

"Thank you, Lord. Would be awkward if I was a woman since you clearly aren't into women."

"I'm not into *you*," she snapped at the same time he shut the water off.

He stuck his head out the bathroom door. His eyes glittered dangerously, temper brewing like a wild storm pushed by the dry line. "You can lie to whomever it is you need to, should it actually be important for them to believe there's nothing between us. But with me?" He narrowed his gaze. "You tell the truth, no matter how much it hurts."

"I didn't know about the letter," she whispered brokenly, twisting her hands together. "And I wasn't trying to use you or your family. I was only trying to keep my business, to keep my people employed. I should have explained that to you, even without the letter. But I was a coward, and I'm sorry."

She saw him coming and stood her ground. He wrapped her in his arms and put one leg around hers to keep her from breaking away. His mouth closed in on hers with a type of dominant possessiveness she'd never experienced but had dreamed of over and over again. With him, only him. "Cade," she breathed.

Their tongues clashed this time, thrusting in a pantomime of sex. She breathed into his mouth, "We have to stop."

He gripped her skull and tilted her head for access to her neck, kissing his way to her jawline and then her neck. "No."

"Cade, stop." This she managed more firmly.

For a split second, he froze. Then, with the superior

control of a man on the edge, he stepped away. "My apologies, Ms. Graystone."

"Call me Emma."

"I'll call you Emma when you kiss me the way you used to."

"I know what I need, Cade, and it's more than great sex with no foreseeable lifespan. I'm the woman who has to have longevity, commitment, certainty. Can you offer that to me? Do you trust me to live this life with you? Do you believe that I will love you and this place as much as you do?"

The emotional vacancy on his face as he turned gutted her. "Good night, Ms. Graystone."

THE DAY OF the wedding dawned bright and clear. Winds were out of the southwest at a very mild seven miles per hour. The high was forecast at seventy-one degrees, and there was a zero percent forecast for rain.

Cade and his brothers dressed at Emma's former cabin following fierce threats of emasculation if any of them set foot in the main house.

He'd just tied his bow tie when Eli came into the bedroom and shut the door. "Cold feet?" Cade teased. "Because if she's going to castrate you for seeing her before the wedding, can you imagine what she'd do if you backed out?"

Eli's wild eyes met his.

"I was kidding," Cade said softly, only to accept the ring box when Eli shoved it at him. "Why are you giving this to me?"

Eli took a shaky breath. "I've already talked to Tyson. He understands." Eli popped his neck. "Why do they make these collars so tight, anyway?"

"To prepare you for marriage?" Cade asked innocently.

"Shut up. You're not helping. This is harder than it was to ask her to marry me."

Concerned, Cade didn't comment. He did, however, wave his hand impatiently for his brother to get on with it.

"Okay, okay." Clearing his throat, he crossed his hands in a military at-rest position. "Cade, we've had our differences. I missed out on a major part of your life I should have been here for." Eli paused and found a place over Cade's shoulder to focus on. "We didn't get on when I first came back, and I get it. But I want you to know that I'm incredibly proud of what you managed to accomplish in spite of my absence." Then he gestured to the ring box. "You've grown into the kind of man I wish I'd had the strength to become. Going into this new phase of my life, I'd be honored as hell if you'd be my best man and stand up there with me to encourage me to do just that."

Words failed Cade. Completely. His throat tightened. Could this kind of emotional response send someone into anaphylactic shock? He closed his eyes and, taking an unsteady breath, nodded. "I'd be honored, Eli." Then he cracked one eye open and glared at his brother. "In the future, I suggest you don't make momentous decisions like this at the last minute. I mean, I could've had a mani/pedi scheduled. Then what would you have done?"

"Flown solo, minus my wingman." Eli tagged him in the shoulder. "Would've sucked."

"Yeah, it was a gamble."

"But you're not going to let me suffer this in silence."

"Suffering in silence isn't, um, my thing." Cade stared

at Eli for a moment before gesturing at the ring box. "Are you sure about this?"

"About what?"

"Me. Wanting me. To be your best man today. It's not conventional, I know, how it all happened. Don't you have friends you'd rather stand up for you?" Cade clutched the ring box with a death grip. "Why me?"

"I want you as my wingman. I want you to stand up before God and all our nosy neighbors, and look fierce if anyone seems like they're going to object when the pastor calls out the option." Then he reached over and took Cade by the bicep, his face serious. "All humor aside?"

Cade nodded, mouth too dry to speak.

"Man, you're my brother." Eli opened his mouth to say more and shook his head, his eyes red, a shimmer of tears catching the light. "You're my brother."

Tears threatened, and Cade only tilted his head back and let the emotional cards fall where they may.

His brother thought a lot of him as a man. But he hadn't been much of a man last night with Emma. She'd deserved some assurances, and he hadn't been able to give them to her.

He'd watched his father turn into a bitter, angry man because of love, and he'd vowed never to become his father. But here was Eli, ready to profess his love and give everything he was and had to Reagan. Did Cade believe Eli would become their old man? No, he was a better man than their father ever had been. And so was Cade.

So he'd put himself out there. He'd make sure she never had to wonder if he'd been coerced or acted out of guilt or whatever other crazy stories she might concoct. She would know that this was where she belonged. With him.

A soft knock sounded on the door, and they both called, "Come in," at the same time.

The door pushed in and Cade stopped breathing. Emma wore a fitted gown of dark chocolate that had been somehow gathered at the sides so it created a draping effect to the knees where it then flared out. She reached behind her for something and Cade couldn't help but gasp. The gown was backless—from the top of her shoulders to the sway of her bottom—*nothing*.

Cade let out a single whistle.

She brought boutonnieres into the room, a pretty flush staining her pale skin. "Stop. You're going to make me self-conscious."

That was fine with him. Maybe then she'd put on a shawl.

Cade stepped toward her. "Will you pin mine on for me?"

She silently moved in close enough he could smell her. Without a word, she pinned his small calla lily boutonniere on his lapel. Then she repeated the same procedure for Eli.

"Where's Tyson?" Cade's voice was gravelly.

Emma laughed, the sound only reinforcing his arousal. "He's on the front porch waiting to escort Reagan 'at the Commander's commanding command.'" She crossed to Eli and took his hand. "She'll be starting down the aisle at exactly one o'clock, so you'd better take your place, Eli."

The eldest Covington paled. "Yeah. Take my place."

She cupped Eli's cheek, and Cade was overcome with such strong emotion for her that he fought the urge to take her free hand, to thank her for comforting his older brother. "She's beautiful, Eli. She's positively vibrating with the intensity of love she has for you."

"You sure?" Eli asked in a rare show of insecurity that made Cade's gaze snap toward his brother.

"I'm more sure of this than anything in my life."

The comment, meant to reassure, cut Cade to the quick. He hadn't been the man she deserved, but he vowed to change for her. Not next week, not tomorrow, not later today, not after the ceremony. *Now.* Today was a day for making vows that lasted lifetimes. Eli and Reagan would make their vows publicly. He'd see to it that he and Emma took theirs however they had to. Days like today, where the heart was entirely sure of itself, shouldn't be squandered.

She left the room, calling out that Eli had fifteen minutes to get to his place in the event hall. Cade was to radio Tyson when Eli was in place. Then the bridal party would start from the house.

With the kind of grace few women possessed, she shut the door behind her and sashayed up the path to the house.

Cade knew because he watched her take every step until she was through the front door.

"You okay?" Eli asked.

"Not really." Cade stuffed his hands in his pants' pockets and loosed a cynical laugh. "Not at all. She's been here days already. I've managed one stolen kiss she told me to stop. I did because I respect her, Eli, but I didn't want to stop. I want her as lost to me as I am to her."

His older brother smiled softly, the gesture full of understanding. "I get it."

"Yeah? Then what do I do about it?" Cade asked with something caught between desperation and demand.

"You up the stakes—for both of you."

An idea took form in Cade's head. It meant putting himself out there, putting his pride on the line, but she'd be forced to respond.

He was all in.

17

THE RADIO BEEPED and Cade's voice, clear and smooth, announced Eli had taken his place.

Emma faced Tyson and Reagan. "Ready?"

Reagan let out a little sob. "Yes, please. I'd begun to worry that time had stopped."

"Not quite," Tyson said with quiet assurance. "It just paused, giving you a moment to breathe."

"Longest breath *ever*," Reagan grumbled as they started from the house and Emma laughed.

"That's how these things go. And in fifteen minutes? It'll all be over. You'll be Mrs. Elijah Covington. All this hype for a fast ceremony, but we've all dreamed about our perfect Prince Charming since we were girls." Emma smiled softly. "You're just lucky enough to be marrying yours."

The three of them made their way to the event hall, arriving to find Cade stationed outside the closed doorway.

Emma frowned. "You're supposed to be inside, standing next to Eli."

"I want to walk you down the aisle."

"What?" she gasped. "No! Get inside and take your place. As maid of honor, I walk alone."

"Not today, Ms. Graystone." He proffered his arm. "Now, we can stand out here arguing where the back half of the hall can probably hear us, or you can take my arm and walk down the aisle with me. I'll make sure you're situated before our beautiful bride takes her stroll down the aisle. Choice is yours."

Emma bit the inside of her cheek, thinking. This wasn't worth dragging the ceremony out over. "I wish you'd mentioned this last night."

"You'd have wiggled out of it." He grasped her right hand and tucked it around his arm before looking at Ty. "Do *not* dance her down the aisle. Eli's about to stroke out as is."

Ty grinned. "I'm on my best behavior."

Cade laughed. "That's what terrifies me. It's then that your most creative ideas are usually generated."

Without further ado, Cade saw Emma inside and the music began to play. They walked down the aisle to the traditional *Cannon in D*, and Cade kept the pace slow and leisurely.

"You look absolutely stunning," he murmured.

Eyes straight ahead, she replied with a terse, "Thanks."

"I mean it, Emma. The sight of you blew me away."

People stared at them as they passed, checking her out as if she was from the "Stranger of the Month" club and needed a thorough examination to ensure her urban aura wouldn't taint the community's supply of single men, Bingo hall or water supply.

"Stop. Talking," she said out the side of her mouth.

"Nah. Most of these folks would think we were stuffy if we didn't chat a little."

Her hand flexed on his arm. "Shh."

Cade grinned as they reached the front of the hall and he deposited her on the second step of the stage.

"*First* step," she hissed.

"Why?" He backed away. "I want to be equal with you in all things."

Her eyes widened at the same time as her lips parted. "What?"

Shaking his head, he took his place across from her and signaled the string quartet.

The music changed, transitioning seamlessly to "Here Comes the Bride" as the minister they'd chosen took center stage and motioned for everyone to stand.

Tyson appeared with Reagan on his arm, looking like the proudest brother-in-law a woman could have. The pair moved down the aisle with effortless grace.

Eli moved, transfixed, to the woman who would be his wife. He couldn't wait for her to get to him but had to go to her, to meet her and bring her the rest of the way. The two brothers and the woman between them met roughly a dozen feet from the stage.

The minister smiled. "An anxious groom is a good sign."

The crowd chuckled.

"Who gives this woman's hand in marriage?" the man called out.

"We, the Covingtons, who have loved her all our lives, stand for her today," Tyson answered.

And so the ceremony went. It was short but moving, and, as predicted, over in fifteen minutes. The minister declared Eli and Reagan man and wife and Emma's sob of happiness and heartbreak was lost to the cheers of the guests as Eli laid a heavy kiss on his new wife.

She *wanted* that. Craved it with everything she was. And she might have had it, but she'd lost it. Lost it because one letter had been buried so deep in a file she hadn't found it.

Oh, he wanted her now. The chemistry between them still existed, hot as ever. But when she'd asked, he hadn't been able to give her anything more. She wanted to be needed for who she was, and she wasn't sure she and Cade would ever transcend the darker part of their history.

Grinning as if they'd won the love lottery, Eli and Reagan nearly sprinted down the hall. The moment the doors closed, a muted but decidedly masculine shout of joy could be heard. Guests laughed and the minister said something, but Emma had eyes only for Cade.

He crossed to her and offered her his arm.

She took it easier this time, allowing him to lead her out of the room and into the dining hall, where the reception would be held.

"What's going on in that mind of yours, Emma?" he asked quietly before they reached the head table, where he helped her into her chair.

She smiled a little too brightly. "Just really happy for Eli and Reagan. It's so amazing when it all comes together like this. Rare…" Her voice trailed off as guests began to file in.

Food and drink were shared, toasts were made and the party was in full swing when Emma couldn't take it anymore. She had to get out of the oppressing happiness that made it near impossible to breathe in Cade's presence. This entire wedding had her fingerprints on it, and none of it would ever be for her.

Tyson, her dance partner at that moment, kissed her cheek when the band's latest country cover ended, and she slipped off the dance floor. She needed air. Distance. A logical means of escape. She'd promised to stay a couple more days, but it wasn't going to happen.

A speaker squawked in protest as the microphone

moved too close to someone's mouth. There were shouts of jovial teasing as the band moved things around.

Her hand was on the door lever when that voice, *Cade's* voice, cut through the crowd and quieted them down. "Stop right there, Ms. Graystone."

Cold settled between her shoulder blades.

"Surely you didn't think you'd just slink off in the early evening hours? Because for all you've been here, I've not had my say."

She couldn't force her numb feet to continue forward, not without giving Cade this moment to balance the scales between them. They needed this for the break between them to be clean. No matter how badly it hurt, it had to happen.

Squaring her shoulders, she moved as gracefully as she could to face him.

He stood on the stage, staring at her rather passively.

"When I first met you, I was pretty sure you were going to be a pain in the ass." The crowd chuckled. "Imagine my surprise when I was right." The crowd chuckled louder.

Her face flamed. "Do tell, Mr. Covington. I don't believe I could leave here without knowing which ass cheek I chafed most. Why, I might never sleep well again for not knowing." The dry response garnered fewer chuckles as people tried to figure out what was going on.

"Let me be perfectly clear, Ms. Graystone. You affected both ass cheeks equally. But more than that? You proved devastating to Lassos & Latigos."

She steeled herself.

"You took one of the Covington brothers out of commission, Ms. Graystone." He tipped the brim of his hat up a fraction. "He couldn't sleep. He couldn't eat. He couldn't think. He couldn't install a window in your cabin that would close properly." He paused. "And he couldn't find the faith necessary on a bright morning to believe a woman of your caliber was innocent of what appeared to be rather black-and-white in front of him." A small hand signal and the band started to play. "I failed you, Emma. I professed to love you, and yet I let the first obstacle in our relationship decimate the house of cards we'd built. I will never be able to apologize enough, so I thought I'd put this out there and humble myself in a way you understand. I sang my mother out of her life at her request. I thought it was the hardest thing I'd ever experience. But you leaving me? That's hurt worse. My heart's demanding I at least try, Emma. But instead of singing you out, I'm going to do my damnedest to sing you right back into my life."

The band began at his nod and he opened his mouth. The magic was instant, the crowd totally silent as he sang Dierks Bentley's "Say You Do."

She began to shiver at the first refrain, shaking her head.

Tyson moved out of the crowd and took her hand, leading her onto the vacant dance floor.

"Don't do this to me, Ty," she whispered raggedly. "I can't survive this again."

"Have a little faith, Emma." He spun her out—and right into Cade's arms.

He handed off the microphone but kept singing, dancing with her in front of everyone.

The song wound down and silence ruled the moment as it seemed everyone waited with bated breath for the result of what was the most heartfelt apology she'd ever witnessed.

Cade stepped away from her and went to one knee, pulling out a blue velvet box and flipping the lid open.

He took a deep breath. "Emmaline Graystone, I have loved you from our first thunderstorm. I thought I could live without you. I thought I could carve out some semblance of life in your absence. I was wrong. Nothing's the same without you. I go through the motions but find no joy in life. You, *you*, are my joy. In everything, you are my heart, the reason I take my next breath, the only sense I can find in life. I can't go another day without that. Without you. Would you do me the greatest honor, Emma, and be my wife?"

The ring he'd bought was a classic diamond solitaire, asscher cut, with trillions on the side, large but not gaudy, set in white gold. It was what she would have picked out for herself if anyone had asked what her tastes were. How he knew her so well in such a short amount of time, she would never understand.

"Knee's beginning to go numb, Emma," Cade said, his tone joking, his eyes filled with desperation.

She looked at him, truly looked at him, and saw everything she'd missed, everything that had been missing, since she left. "I want to live here."

"I don't want to live in New York, so that's fine."

"I want a house of our own."

"Done," he answered.

"All the windows have to work."

"You're pushing your luck, Emma," he growled. "I'll give you any damn thing you want if you'll just say yes."

"Yes," she whispered.

The crowd erupted in a cheer. Shouted congratulations were thrown at them as he tenderly placed the ring on her finger, and then exploded off the floor, pulling her into his arms and kissing her with unrestrained passion despite their audience.

"Your business?" he murmured against her lips.

"In the process of being sold to a group of investors headed up by my personal assistant." She grinned.

"I love you, Emma." Cade dipped his head and kissed her again, softer this time. "Be my wife."

"Only if you're offering forever."

"Nothing else would ever be enough," he said gruffly, pulling her into a slow waltz step as the band struck up their next cover song. "I'll never have enough of you." He led her around the floor slowly, his gaze loving. "When does this 'forever' start?"

"When the time's right," she whispered.

His brow creased. "And that would be when?"

"Now."

* * * * *

If you like fun, sexy and steamy stories with strong heroines and irresistible heroes, you'll love THE HARDER YOU FALL by New York Times *bestselling author Gena Showalter—featuring Jessie Kay Dillon and Lincoln West, the sexy bachelor who's breaking all his rules for this rowdy Southern belle...*

Turn the page for a sneak peek at THE HARDER YOU FALL!

WEST HAD BROUGHT a date.

The realization hit Jessie Kay like a bolt of lightning in a freak storm. Great! Wonderful! While she'd opted not to bring Daniel, and thus make West the only single person present—and embarrassingly alone—he'd chosen his next two-month "relationship" and hung Jessie Kay out to dry.

Hidden in the back of the sanctuary, Jessie Kay stood in the doorway used by church personnel and scowled. Harlow had asked for—cough, banshee-screeched, cough—a status report. Jessie Kay had abandoned her precious curling iron in order to sneak a peek at the guys.

Now she pulled her phone out of the pocket in her dress to text Daniel. Oops. She'd missed a text.

Sunny: Party 2nite?????

She made a mental note to respond to Sunny later and drafted her note to Daniel.

I'm at the church. How fast can you get here? I need a friend/date for Harlow's wedding

A response didn't come right away. She knew he'd gone on a date last night and the girl had stayed the night with him. How did she know? Because he'd texted Jessie Kay to ask how early he could give the snoring girl the boot.

Sooo glad I never hooked up with him.

Finally, a vibration signaled a response.

Any other time I'd race to your rescue, even though weddings are snorefests. Today I'm in the city on a job

He'd started some kind of high-risk security firm with a few of his Army buddies.

Her: Fine. You suck. I clearly need to rethink our friendship

Daniel: I'll make it up to you, swear. Want to have dinner later???

She slid her phone back in place without responding, adding his name to her mental note. If he wasn't going to ignore his responsibilities whenever she had a minor need, he deserved to suffer for a little while.

Of its own accord, Jessie Kay's gaze returned to West. The past week, she'd seen him only twice. Both times, she'd gone to the farmhouse to help her sister with sandwiches and casseroles, and he'd taken one look at her, grabbed his keys and driven off.

Would it have killed him to acknowledge her presence by calling her by some hateful name, per usual? After all, he'd had the nerve to flirt with her at the diner, to look at her as if she'd stripped naked and begged him to have *her* for dessert. And now he ignored her? Men! This one in particular.

Her irritation grew as he introduced his date to Kenna Starr and her fiancé, Dane Michaelson. Kenna was a stunning redhead who'd always been Brook Lynn's partner in crime. The girl who'd done what Jessie Kay had not, saving her sister every time she'd gotten into trouble.

Next up was an introduction to Daphne Roberts, the mother of Jase's nine-year-old daughter, Hope, then Brad Lintz, Daphne's boyfriend.

Jase and Beck joined the happy group, but the brunette never looked away from West, as if he was speaking the good Lord's gospel. Her adoration was palpable.

A sharp pang had Jessie Kay clutching her chest. *Too young for a heart attack.*

Indigestion?

Yeah. Had to be.

The couple should have looked odd together. West was too tall and the brunette was far too short for him. A skyscraper next to a one-story house. But somehow, despite their height difference, the two actually complemented each other.

And really, the girl's adoration had to be good for West, buoying him the way Daniel's praise often buoyed Jessie Kay. Only on a much higher level, considering the girl was more than a friend to West.

Deep down, Jessie Kay was actually…happy for West. As crappy as his childhood had been, he deserved a nice slice of contentment.

Look at me, acting like a big girl and crap.

When West wrapped his arm around the brunette's waist, drawing her closer, Jessie Kay's nails dug into her palms.

I'm happy for him, remember? Besides, big girls

didn't want to push other women in front of a speeding bus.

Jessie Kay's phone buzzed. Another text. This one from Brook Lynn.

Hurry! Bridezilla is on a rampage!!!

Her: Tell her the guys look amazing in their tuxes—no stains or tears yet—and the room is gorgeous. Or just tell her NOTHING HAS FREAKING CHANGED

The foster bros had gone all out even though the ceremony was to be a small and intimate affair. There were red and white roses at the corner of every pew, and in front of the pulpit was an ivory arch with wispy jewel-encrusted lace.

With a sigh, she added an adorable smiley face to her message, because it was cute and it said *I'm not yelling at you. My temper is not engaged.*

Send.

Brook Lynn: Harlow wants a play-by-play of the action

Fine.

Beck is now speaking w/Pastor Washington. Jase, Dane, Kenna, Daphne & Brad are engaged in conversation, while Hope is playing w/ her doll on the floor. Happy?

She didn't add that West was focused on the stunning brunette, who was still clinging to his side.

The girl…she had a familiar face—*where have I seen her?*—and a body so finely honed Jessie Kay wanted to stuff a few thousand Twinkies down her throat just to make it fair for the rest of the female population. Her designer dress was made of ebony silk and hugged her curves like a besotted lover.

Like West would be doing tonight?

Grinding her teeth, Jessie Kay slid her gaze over her own gown. One she'd sewn in her spare time. Not bad—actually kind of awesome—but compared to Great Bod's delicious apple it was a rotten orange.

A wave of jealousy swept over her. Dang it! Jealousy was stupid. Jessie Kay was no can of dog food in the looks department. In fact, she was well able to hold her own against anyone, anywhere, anytime. But…but…

A lot of baggage came with her.

West suddenly stiffened, as if he knew he was being watched. He turned. Her heart slamming against her ribs with enough force to break free and escape, she darted into Harlow's bridal chamber—the choir room.

Harlow finished curling her thick mass of hair as Brook Lynn gave her lips a final swipe of gloss.

"Welcome to my nightmare," Jessie Kay announced. "I might as well put in rollers, pull on a pair of mom jeans and buy ten thousand cats." Cats! Want! "I'm officially an old maid without any decent prospects."

Brook Lynn wrinkled her brow. "What are you talking about?"

"Everyone is here, including West and his date. I'm the only single person in our group, which means you guys have to set me up with your favorite guy friends. Obviously I'm looking for a nine or ten. Make it happen. Please and thank you."

Harlow went still. "West brought a date? Who is it?"

Had a curl of steam just risen from her nostrils? "Just some girl."

Harlow pressed her hands against a stomach that had to be dancing with nerves. "I don't want *just some girl* at my first wedding."

"You planning your divorce to Beck already?"

Harlow scowled at her. "Not funny. You know we're planning a larger ceremony next year."

Jessie Kay raised her hands, palms out. "You're right, you're right. And you totally convinced me. I'll kick the bitch out pronto." *And I'll love every second of it—on Harlow's behalf.*

"No. No. I don't want a scene." Stomping her foot, Harlow added, "What was West thinking? He's ruined *everything.*"

Ooo-kay. A wee bit dramatic, maybe. "I doubt he was thinking at all. If that boy ever had an idea, it surely died of loneliness." Too much? "Anyway. I'm sure you could use a glass or six of champagne. I'll open the bottle for us—for you. You're welcome."

A wrist corsage hit her square in the chest.

"This is *my* day, Jessica Dillon." Harlow thumped her chest. "Mine! You will remain stone-cold sober, or I will remove your head, place it on a stick and wave it around while your sister sobs over your bleeding corpse."

Wow. "That's pretty specific, but I feel you. No alcohol for me, ma'am." She gave a jaunty salute. "I mean, no alcohol for me, Miss Bridezilla, sir."

"Ha-ha." Harlow morphed from fire-breathing dragon to fairy-tale princess in an instant, twirling in a circle. "Now stop messing around and tell me how amazing I look. And don't hesitate to use words like *exquisite* and *magical.*"

The hair at her temples had been pulled back, but the rest hung to her elbows in waves so dark they glimmered blue in the light. The gown had capped sleeves and a straight bustline with a cinched-in waist and pleats that flowed all the way to the floor, covering the sensible flats she'd chosen based on West's advice. "You look... exquisitely magical."

"Magically exquisite," Brook Lynn said with a nod.

"My scars aren't hideous?" Self-conscious, Harlow smoothed a hand over the multitude of jagged pink lines running between her breasts, courtesy of an attack she'd miraculously survived as a teenage girl.

"Are you kidding? Those scars make you look bad-ass." Jessie Kay curled a few more pieces of hair, adding, "I'm bummed my skin is so flawless."

Harlow snorted. "Yes, let's shed a tear for you."

Jessie Kay gave her sister the stink eye. "You better not be like this for your wedding. I won't survive two of you."

Brook Lynn held up her well-manicured hands, all innocence.

"Well." She glanced at a wristwatch she wasn't wearing, doing her best impression of West. "We've got twenty minutes before the festivities kick off. Need anything?"

Harlow's hands returned to her stomach, the color draining from her cheeks in a hurry. "Yes. Beck."

Blinking, certain she'd misheard, she fired off a quick "Excuse me?" Heck. Deck. Neck. Certainly not Beck. "Grooms aren't supposed to see—"

"I need Beck." Harlow stomped her foot. *"Now."*

"Have you changed your mind?" Brook Lynn asked. "If so, we'll—"

"No, no. Nothing like that." Harlow launched into a quick pace, marching back and forth through the room.

"I just… I need to see him. He hates change, and this is the biggest one of all, and I need to talk to him before I totally. Flip. Out. Okay? All right?"

"This isn't that big a change, honey. Not really." Who would have guessed Jessie Kay would be a voice of reason in a situation like this. Or *any* situation? "You guys live together already."

"Beck!" she insisted. "Beck, Beck, Beck."

"Temper tantrums are not attractive." Jessie Kay shared a concerned look with her sister, who nodded. "All right. One Beck coming up." As fast as her heels would allow, she made her way back to the sanctuary.

She purposely avoided West's general direction, focusing only on the groom. "Harlow has decided to throw millions of years' worth of tradition out the window. She wants to see you without delay. Are you wearing a cup? I'd wear a cup. Good luck."

He'd been in the middle of a conversation with Jase, and like Harlow, he quickly paled. "Is something wrong with her?" He didn't stick around for an answer, rushing past Jessie Kay without actually judging the distance between them, almost knocking her over.

As she stumbled, West flew over and latched on to her wrist to help steady her. The contact nearly buckled her knees. His hands were calloused, his fingers firm. His strength unparalleled and his skin hot enough to burn. Electric tingles rushed through her, the world around her fading from existence until they were the only two people in existence.

Fighting for every breath, she stared up at him. His gaze dropped to her lips and narrowed, his focus savagely carnal and primal in its possessiveness, as if he saw nothing else, either—wanted nothing and no one else ever. But as he slowly lowered his arm and stepped away from her, the world snapped back into motion.

The bastard brought a date.

Right. She cleared her throat, embarrassed by the force of her reaction to him. "Thanks."

A muscle jumped in his jaw. A sign of anger? "May I speak with you privately?"

Uh… "Why?"

"Please."

What the what now? Had Lincoln West actually said the word *please* to her? *Her?* "Whatever you have to say to me—" an insult, no doubt "—can wait. You should return to your flavor of the year." Opting for honesty, she grudgingly added, "You guys look good together."

The muscle jumped again, harder, faster. "You think we look good together?"

"Very much so." Two perfect people. "I'm not being sarcastic, if that's what you're getting at. Who is she?"

"Monica Gentry. Fitness guru based in the city."

Well. That explained the sense of familiarity. And the body. Jessie Kay had once briefly considered thinking about exercising along with Monica's video. Then she'd found a bag of KIT KAT Minis and the insane idea went back to hell, where it belonged. "She's a good choice for you. Beautiful. Successful. Driven. And despite what you think about me, despite the animosity between us, I want you happy."

And not just because of his crappy childhood, she realized. He was a part of her family, for better or worse. A girl made exceptions for family. Even the douche bags.

His eyes narrowed to tiny slits. "We're going to speak privately, Jessie Kay, whether you agree or not. The only decision you need to make is whether or not you'll walk. I'm more than willing to carry you."

A girl also had the right to smack family. "You're just going to tell me to change my hideous dress, and I'm going to tell you I'm fixing to cancel your birth certificate."

When Harlow had proclaimed *Wear whatever you want*, Jessie Kay had done just that, creating a bloodred, off-the-shoulder, pencil-skirt dress that molded to her curves like a second skin...made from leftover material for drapes.

Scarlett O'Hara has nothing on me!

Jessie Kay was proud of her work, but she wasn't blind to its flaws. Knotted threads in the seams. Years had passed since she'd sewn anything, and her skills were rusty.

West gave her another once—twice—over as fire smoldered in his eyes. "Why would I tell you to change?" His voice dipped, nothing but smoke and gravel. "You and that dress are a fantasy come true."

Uh, what the what now? Had Lincoln West just called her *a fantasy*?

Almost can't process...

"Maybe you should take me to the ER, West. I think I just had a brain aneurysm." She rubbed her temples. "I'm hallucinating."

"Such a funny girl." He ran his tongue over his teeth, snatched her hand and while Monica called his name, dragged Jessie Kay to a small room in back. A cleaning closet, the air sharp with antiseptic. What little space was available was consumed by overstuffed shelves.

"When did you decide to switch careers and become a caveman?" she asked.

"When you decided to switch careers and become a femme fatale."

Have mercy on my soul.

He released her to run his fingers through his hair, leaving the strands in sexy spikes around his head. "Listen. I owe you an apology for the way I've treated you in the past. The way I've acted today. I shouldn't have manhandled you, and I'm very sorry."

Her eyes widened. Seriously, what the heck had happened to this man? In five minutes, he'd upended everything she'd come to expect from him.

And he wasn't done! "I'm sorry for every hurtful thing I've ever said to you. I'm sorry for making you feel bad about who you are and what you've done. I'm sorry—"

"Stop. Just stop." She placed her hands over her ears in case he failed to heed her order. "I don't understand what's happening."

He gently removed her hands and held on tight to her wrists. "What's happening? I'm owning my mistakes and hoping you're in a forgiving mood."

"You want to be my friend?" The words squeaked from her.

"I…do."

Why the hesitation? "Here's the problem. You're a dog and I'm a cat, and we're never going to get along."

One corner of his mouth quirked with lazy amusement, causing a flutter to skitter through her pulse. "I think you're wrong…kitten."

Kitten. A freakishly adorable nickname, and absolutely perfect for her. But also absolutely unexpected.

Oh, she'd known he'd give her one sooner or later. He and his friends enjoyed renaming the women in their lives. Jase always called Brook Lynn "angel" and Beck called Harlow everything from "beauty" to "hag," her initials. Well, HAG prewedding. But Jessie Kay had prepared herself for "demoness" or the always classic "bitch."

"Dogs and cats can be friends," he said, "especially when the dog minds his manners. I promise you, things will be different from now on."

"Well." Reeling, she could come up with no witty reply. "We could try, I guess."

"Good." His gaze dropped to her lips, heated a few more degrees. "Now all we have to do is decide what kind of friends we should be."

Her heart started kicking up a fuss all over again, breath abandoning her lungs. "What do you mean?"

"Text frequently? Call each other occasionally? Only speak when we're with our other friends?" He backed her into a shelf and cans rattled, threatening to fall. "Or should we be friends with benefits?"

The tingles returned, sweeping over her skin and sinking deep, deep into bone. Her entire body ached with sudden need and it was so powerful it nearly felled her. How long since a man had focused the full scope of his masculinity on her? Too long and never like this. Somehow West had reduced her to a quivering mess of femininity and whoremones.

"I vote...we only speak when we're with our other friends," she said, embarrassed by the breathless tremor in her voice.

"What if I want all of it?" He placed his hands at her temples and several of the cans rolled to the floor. "The texts, the calls...and the benefits."

"No?" A question? Really? "No to the last. You have a date."

He scowled at her as if *she'd* done something wrong. "See, that's the real problem, kitten. I don't want her. I want you."

WEST CALLED HIMSELF a thousand kinds of fool. He'd planned to apologize, return to the sanctuary, witness his friend's wedding and start the countdown with Monica. The moment he'd gotten Jessie Kay inside the closet, her pecans-and-cinnamon scent in his nose, those plans burned to ash. Only one thing mattered.

Getting his hands on her.

From day one, she'd been a vertical g-force too strong to deny, pulling, pulling, *pulling* him into a bottomless vortex. He'd fought it every minute of every day since meeting her, and he'd gotten nowhere fast. Why not give in? Stop the madness?

Just once...

"We've been dancing around this for months," he said. "I'm scum for picking here and now to hash this out with you, and I'll care tomorrow. Right now, I think it's time we did something about our feelings."

"I don't..." She began to soften against him, only to snap to attention. "No. Absolutely not. I can't."

"You *won't*." But *I can change your mind...*

She nibbled on her bottom lip.

Something he would kill to do. So he did it. He leaned into her, caught her bottom lip between his teeth and ran the plump morsel through. "Do you want me, Jessie Kay?"

Her eyes closed for a moment, a shiver rocking her. "You say you'll care tomorrow, so I'll give you an answer then. As for today, I... I... I'm leaving." But she made no effort to move away, and he knew. She did want him. As badly as he wanted her. "Yes. Leaving. Any moment now..."

Acting without thought—purely on instinct—he placed his hands on her waist and pressed her against the hard line of his body. "I want you to stay. I want you, period."

"West." The new tremor in her voice injected his every masculine instinct with adrenaline, jacking him up. "You said it yourself. You're scum. This is wrong."

Anticipation raced denial to the tip of his tongue, and won by a photo finish. "Do you care?" He caressed his way to her ass and cupped the perfect globes, then urged her forward to rub her against the long length of his erection. The woman who'd tormented his days and invaded his dreams moaned a decadent sound of satisfaction and it did something to him. Made his need for her *worse*.

She wasn't what he should want, but somehow she'd become everything he could not resist, and he was tired, so damn tired, of walking, hell, running away from her.

"Do you?" he insisted. "Say yes, and *I'll* be the one to leave. I don't want you to regret this." He wanted her desperate for more.

She looked away from him, licked her lips. "Right at this moment? No. I don't care." As soft as a whisper.

Triumph filled him, his clasp on her tightening.

"But tomorrow..." she added.

Yes. Tomorrow. He wasn't the only one who'd been running from the sizzle between them, but today, with her admission ringing in his ears, he wasn't letting her get away. One look at her, that's all it had taken to ruin his plans. Now she would pay the price. Now she would make everything better.

"I *will* regret it," she said. "This is a mistake I've made too many times in the past."

Different emotions played over her features. Features so delicate he was consumed by the need to protect her from anything and anyone...but himself.

He saw misery, desire, fear, regret, hope and anger. The anger concerned him. This Southern belle could knock a man's testicles into his throat with a single swipe of her knee. Even still, West didn't walk away.

"For all we know, the world will end tomorrow. Let's focus on today. You tell me what you want me to do," he said, nuzzling his nose against her cheek, "and I'll do it."

More tremors rocked her. She traced her delicate hands up his tie and gave the knot a little shake, an action that was sexy, sweet and wicked all at once. "I want you...to go back to your date. You and I, we'll be friends as agreed, and we'll pretend this never happened." She pushed him, but he didn't budge.

His date. Yeah, he'd forgotten about Monica before Jessie Kay had mentioned her a few minutes ago. But then, he'd gotten used to forgetting everything whenever the luscious blonde entered a room. Everything about her consumed every part of him, and it was more than irritating, it was a sickness to be cured, an obstacle to be overcome and an addiction to be avoided. If they did this, he would suffer from his own regrets, but there was no question he would love the ride.

He bunched up the hem of her skirt, his fingers brushing the silken heat of her bare thigh. Her breath hitched, driving him wild. "You've told me what you *think* you should want me to do." He rasped the words against her mouth, hovering over her, not touching her but teasing with what could be. "Now tell me what you really want me to do."

Navy blues peered up at him, beseeching; the fight drained out of her, leaving only need and raw vulnerability. "I'm only using you for sex—said no guy ever. But that's what you're going to do. Isn't it? You're going to use me and lose me, just like the others."

Her features were utterly *ravaged*, and in that moment, he hated himself. Because she was right. Whether he took her for a single night or every night for two months, the end result would be the same. No matter how much it hurt her—no matter how much it hurt *him*—he would walk away.

Don't miss a single story in
THE ORIGINAL HEARTBREAKERS *series:*
"THE ONE YOU WANT" (novella)
THE CLOSER YOU COME
THE HOTTER YOU BURN
THE HARDER YOU FALL

*Available now from Gena Showalter
and HQN Books!*

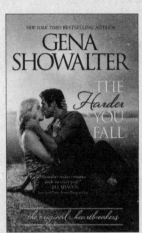

$7.99 U.S./$9.99 CAN.

EXCLUSIVE
Limited time offer!

$1.⁰⁰ OFF

New York Times bestselling author
GENA SHOWALTER

is back with another sizzling
Original Heartbreakers story featuring
an aloof bad boy and the rowdy
Southern belle who rocks his world...

THE *Harder* YOU FALL

Available November 24, 2015.
Pick up your copy today!

HQN™

$1.⁰⁰ OFF   the purchase price of
THE HARDER YOU FALL by Gena Showalter.

Offer valid from November 24, 2015, to December 31, 2015.
Redeemable at participating retail outlets. Not redeemable at Barnes & Noble.
Limit one coupon per purchase. Valid in the U.S.A. and Canada only.

52613047

5 65373 00076 2   (8100)0 12095

® and ™ are trademarks owned and used by the trademark owner and/or its licensee.

© 2015 Harlequin Enterprises Limited

PHGS1215COUP

SPECIAL EXCERPT FROM

⬡HARLEQUIN® *Blaze*

*When Maddie Holmes first meets Mason Black she has
no idea he's a Navy SEAL on an undercover mission…
but she's about to find out all his secrets!*

Read on for a sneak preview of
PLEASING HER SEAL *by* **Anne Marsh**
part of Harlequin Blaze's
UNIFORMLY HOT! *miniseries.*

Fantasy Island advertised itself as an idyllic slice of
paradise located on the Caribbean Sea—the perfect place
for a destination wedding or honeymoon. The elegant type
on the resort brochure promised barefoot luxury, discreet
hedonism and complete wish fulfillment. Maddie's job
was to translate those naughty promises into sexy web
copy that would drive traffic to her blog and fill her bank
account with much-needed advertising dollars.

The summit beckoned, and she stepped out into a
small clearing overlooking the ocean.

"Good view?" At the sound of the deep male voice
behind her, Maddie flinched, arms and legs jerking
in shock. Her camera flew forward as she scrambled
backward.

Strong male fingers fastened around her wrist. Pan-
icked, she grabbed her croissant and lobbed it at the guy,
followed by her coffee. He cursed and dodged.

"It's not a good day to jump without a chute." He
tugged her away from the edge of the lookout, and she
got her first good look at him. Not a stranger. *Okay, then.*

HBEXP1215

Her heart banged hard against her rib cage, pummeling her lungs, before settling back into a more normal rhythm. *Mason*. Mason I-Can't-Be-Bothered-To-Tell-You-My-Last-Name-But-I'm-A-Stud. He led the cooking classes by the pool. She'd written him off as good-looking but aloof, not certain if she'd spotted a spark of potential interest in his dark eyes. Wishful thinking or dating potential—it was probably a moot point now, since she'd just pegged him with her mocha.

He didn't seem pissed off. On the contrary, he simply rocked back on his haunches, hands held out in front of him. *I come in peace*, she thought, fortunately too out of breath to giggle. The side of his shirt sported a dark stain from her coffee. Oh, goody. She'd actually scalded him. Way to make an impression on a poor, innocent guy. This was why her dating life sucked.

She tried to wheeze out an apology, but he shook his head.

"I scared you."

"You think?"

"That wasn't my intention." The look on his face was part chagrin, part repentance. Worked for her.

"I'll put a bell around your neck." Where had he learned to move so quietly?

"Why don't we start over?" He stuck out a hand. A big, masculine, slightly muddy hand. She probably shouldn't want to seize his fingers like a lifeline. "I'm Mason Black."

Don't miss PLEASING HER SEAL by Anne Marsh, available January 2016 wherever Harlequin® Blaze® books and ebooks are sold.

www.Harlequin.com

REQUEST YOUR FREE BOOKS!
2 FREE NOVELS PLUS 2 FREE GIFTS!

⊞ HARLEQUIN®

Blaze

red-hot reads!

YES! Please send me 2 FREE Harlequin® Blaze® novels and my 2 FREE gifts (gifts are worth about $10). After receiving them, if I don't wish to receive any more books, I can return the shipping statement marked "cancel." If I don't cancel, I will receive 4 brand-new novels every month and be billed just $4.74 per book in the U.S. or $5.21 per book in Canada. That's a savings of at least 14% off the cover price. It's quite a bargain. Shipping and handling is just 50¢ per book in the U.S. and 75¢ per book in Canada.* I understand that accepting the 2 free books and gifts places me under no obligation to buy anything. I can always return a shipment and cancel at any time. Even if I never buy another book, the two free books and gifts are mine to keep forever.

150/350 HDN GH2D

Name	(PLEASE PRINT)	
Address		Apt. #
City	State/Prov.	Zip/Postal Code

Signature (if under 18, a parent or guardian must sign)

Mail to the **Reader Service:**
IN U.S.A.: P.O. Box 1867, Buffalo, NY 14240-1867
IN CANADA: P.O. Box 609, Fort Erie, Ontario L2A 5X3

Want to try two free books from another line?
Call 1-800-873-8635 or visit www.ReaderService.com.

* Terms and prices subject to change without notice. Prices do not include applicable taxes. Sales tax applicable in N.Y. Canadian residents will be charged applicable taxes. Offer not valid in Quebec. This offer is limited to one order per household. Not valid for current subscribers to Harlequin Blaze books. All orders subject to credit approval. Credit or debit balances in a customer's account(s) may be offset by any other outstanding balance owed by or to the customer. Please allow 4 to 6 weeks for delivery. Offer available while quantities last.

Your Privacy—The Reader Service is committed to protecting your privacy. Our Privacy Policy is available online at www.ReaderService.com or upon request from the Reader Service.

We make a portion of our mailing list available to reputable third parties that offer products we believe may interest you. If you prefer that we not exchange your name with third parties, or if you wish to clarify or modify your communication preferences, please visit us at www.ReaderService.com/consumerschoice or write to us at Reader Service Preference Service, P.O. Box 9062, Buffalo, NY 14240-9062. Include your complete name and address.

Turn your love of reading into rewards you'll love with
Harlequin My Rewards

**Join for FREE today at
www.HarlequinMyRewards.com**

Earn **FREE BOOKS** of your choice.

Experience **EXCLUSIVE OFFERS** and contests.

Enjoy **BOOK RECOMMENDATIONS**
selected just for you.

PLUS! Sign up now
and get **500** points
right away!

Earn **FREE** REWARDS
Join Today!
HarlequinMyRewards.com

MYR16R